Albert Smith

To China and Back

SALZWASSER
VERLAG

Albert Smith

To China and Back

Reprint of the original, first published in 1859.

1st Edition 2023 | ISBN: 978-3-37513-532-4

Verlag (Publisher): Salzwasser Verlag GmbH, Zeilweg 44, 60439 Frankfurt, Deutschland
Vertretungsberechtigt (Authorized to represent): E. Roepke, Zeilweg 44, 60439 Frankfurt, Deutschland
Druck (Print): Books on Demand GmbH, In de Tarpen 42, 22848 Norderstedt, Deutschland

TO

CHINA AND BACK:

BEING

A DIARY KEPT, OUT AND HOME,

BY

ALBERT SMITH.

PUBLISHED FOR THE AUTHOR,
AND TO BE HAD OF
MESSRS. CHAPMAN & HALL, 193, PICCADILLY;
AT THE
EGYPTIAN HALL;
OF ALL BOOKSELLERS, AND AT ALL RAILWAY STATIONS.
Price One Shilling.

PREFACE.

THIS little book is really what it is called—"A Diary kept Out and Home," and nothing more : such parts only being omitted as were of a private or domestic nature. It is intended as a companion to my Lecture, into the two hours of which I have so much to condense, that I can scarcely keep the thread of the voyage and incidents satisfactorily together ; and I hope it will agreeably fill up these " solutions of continuity."

When my audience recollect that I nearly saw the London season of 1858 to its close, and then went to China and back, returning, as I promised them, in July, " with the Cattle-Show and Pantomimes," after a voyage of twenty thousand miles, they must allow that a superficial view only of this strange country could be attempted. The whole journey was such a spasm, that I forgive those who doubted the fact of my having undertaken it. An esteemed friend, in the Peninsular and Oriental Company, told me he had been asked, more than once, if I really *had* gone ; or whether I had hidden myself in the Alps, and there compiled my entertainment from the books and hints of other travellers !

I hope some of my old friends at Hong Kong and Canton, who so puzzled themselves about "what I could possibly find interesting out there, as I did not care about trade," will see that to a stranger there are yet a few points to interest, beyond opium, silk, tea, markets, exchange, and gunny-bags. The pure business mind is the same everywhere—whether in the Commercial Room of the Yorkshire inn, or Compradorial Godown of the tropics. The odd things connected with Buddhist worship possessed greater attraction for me than the other absorbing religion of folks living in China—the Almighty Dollar.

Should my readers wish to know more about many of the points lightly touched on in this *brochure*, I hope Mr. Wingrove Cooke will not be offended when I state that his charming work on China, is to my thinking, the first practically graphic book that has been published on this most interesting portion of the world.

NORTH END LODGE,

WALHAM GREEN, S.W.,

March, 1859

TO CHINA AND BACK.

Saturday, July 17, 1858.—This morning, about half-past five, the Peninsular and Oriental Company's fine steam-ship, *Pera*, Captain Jamieson, entered the harbour of Alexandria, piloted in by an Arab, grubbily resplendent with the dirty finery that characterises the Eastern races generally.

Immediately a crowd of swarthy beings still dirtier swarmed up the sides and about the deck and lower rigging, climbing, squabbling, and jabbering like so many apes; and the business of landing the Overland Mail commenced. These fellows were dressed in seedy blue tronsers, tight at the ancles—peg-top fashion—and very old blue blouse-looking tunics, tied round the waist with a filthy remnant of a shawl. They also wore generally a washed-out, perspirationed, sun-blanched fez, and were mostly one-eyed. A Prancer on board termed them "picturesque creatures." She was not picturesque herself, for she must have been five-and-forty, yet wore one of those charming hats which should only belong to youth and beauty. But she was lively—the dear old kitten—and had pretty little ways, and was sometimes particular, because she was "without a chaperon."

About seven the Pacha's sister embarked in a large white steamer, for a visit to Constantinople, amidst the firing of guns from all the Egyptian frigates in the harbour. Except for this purpose, the Pacha's navy is useless. The noise and smoke gave one a very good idea of what it must be to be in action. The mails and luggage were soon disembarked by the Arabs, and then we all went from the pier, on a hot sandy unfinished road, to the railway; having enough to do to keep our hand-baggage from being seized by the boys, hold our umbrellas over our heads, and drive the flies from the corners of our eyes, where they love to nestle. The train for Cairo started at nine. Men were selling cakes and lemonade, as well as white coverings for the hats, and little fans of matting to blow away the flies with. The carriages were all in the English style, with London makers' names.

The view from the railway is very monotonous. It is interesting just as you leave Alexandria to look at its domes and minarets, with Pompey's Pillar on the hill, and the gardens of dates, plantains, and prickly pears; but all this quickly merges into a tawny dried-up desert, with distant glimpses of the villas on the Mahmoudieh canal, which you soon leave on the left. A shed of board and matting is passed with the sign of "Wood's Railway Tavern." For nearly the whole distance a bridle road runs parallel with the line, which is a single one, and separated from it by a ditch. Along this road many men passed on donkeys, sitting well back behind; some, also, were on camels, and

some on magnificent high-bred horses. About one we crossed the
Nile in an inconvenient little steamer. The luggage went across a
pile bridge, but passengers have not passed it since the accident to the
young Pacha a year ago, when he was pushed from it, in his carriage,
into the Nile, and there drowned.

On the other side of this ferry was the Refreshment Station, for
which we had received a ticket on paying our fares. It was a big
barn-looking place, with a doubtful *cuisine*. The chief dish, as indeed
it was all along the desert to Suez, was Irish stew—a secret compound
containing bones, onions, and flies, with shreds of unknown animal
matter. But there was good pale ale, brandy, soda-water, and champagne; and, considering all things, at fair prices. Outside I bought a
very large melon, nearly as big as my head, for twopence.

It was at this place we first heard the terrible details of the Djedda
massacre; and an Egyptian officer, who spoke French, told us that
the Bedouins were coming up the Red Sea, in forty boats, to take
Suez, and that it was also their intention to plunder the mail and
murder the passengers, in consequence of which the Pacha had dispatched some soldiers to Suez as a guard. This was unpleasant news,
and we all naturally felt rather anxious.

We reached Cairo at five, and the usual scramble to get to Shepheard's Hotel before the rest commenced. I was one of the first, and
secured a large airy room looking over the garden, containing the tree
under which General Kleber was assassinated at the revolt of Cairo.
I had some little talk about the bad news with Mr. Roberts, who
manages the house in Shepheard's absence. He feared there was
certainly some truth in what we had heard; but he had not said anything about it for fear of alarming the passengers. I went, after
dinner, with Mr. Badger, the resident clergyman at Aden, to call on
Mr. Ayrton, who is in the confidence of the Pacha, and lives here quite
in Egyptian style. He went over all the details of the massacre, from
the depositions; and the report of the troubled state of the coasts of
the Red Sea did not improve our misgivings. At eight o'clock the
homeward-bound mail came in from China and India, with the news
of poor Dr. Turnbull's murder, in that affair of the White Cloud
Mountains, off Canton. The passengers had heard what we had, at
Suez, but found soldiers there, and the town tranquil. I had little
time for a stroll about Cairo, which I much regretted, for it has always
been to me my greatest travelling treat. I consider it the most
charmingly picturesque city I have ever visited—a lively moving
embodiment of the "Arabian Nights' Entertainments." But there
still appeared to be the same people in the same coffee-houses, listening
with the same attention to the same hunchbacks telling the same
stories; and the same confusion of camels, donkeys, slaves, processions,
horsemen, and veiled women in its narrow thoroughfares, as delighted
me so much ten years ago. And tourists can now "do" Cairo and the
Pyramids, out and home, in under three weeks.

Sunday, 18*th*.—The thermometer stood all night in my bedroom at
89°, and the heat was so great, with all the windows open, that I
scarcely slept at all. They called me at three, when it was nearly dark,
and as nobody else stirred for another half-hour, I had but a dull time
of it, peering out of the window as the day opened over the city.

Heavy drops of dew kept falling from Kleber's tree, and tumbling from leaf to leaf till they reached the ground; and, with a combined noise of dogs fighting, cocks crowing, and crows cawing, merging into the cries and squabbles of the people, Cairo gradually woke into life. We started, in omnibuses, at half-past four, having really a difficulty in driving clear of the multitudes of people lying about the roads still asleep. When we got to the railway nobody was up, or in command, so we took possession of the carriages ourselves, and commenced a grand general British grumble, which lasted until half-past six, when we really did start. At eight o'clock the train shunted into a siding, and kept us there for an hour and a half, waiting for another train to pass, which was telegraphed from Suez. There was a little solitary telegraphic office here, with a lonely clerk, and small bivouac of Bedouins on the other side the rail. He came to beg an English news-paper—"one ever so old would do !" I never had imagined so dismal a position—a telegraph clerk, with nothing to do, in the middle of a desert ! We got half baked in the train, and very tired of waiting; but a dozen young surgeons, bound for India, started a game which soon became popular. They got a skeleton of a camel, and set it up on its haunches, putting a small sum of money on the skull, and thus forming a cock-shy. It was past two in the afternoon when we got to the end of the railway, and we were then about sixteen miles from Suez. Here was another large refreshment barrack, with more nasty things to repress one's appetite; and the flies were worse than ever.

We now started in the vans, each with two horses—leaders—and two mules. The animals were only half-broken, and sometimes the leaders would turn right round and look in at the windows. There was no road but that which the dead camels marked; and we bumped and jolted over the stones—galloping, jibbing, and stopping—melted with the heat, gasping with thirst, powdered with dust worse than on a return from the Derby, and still stormed by the flies beyond all endurance. We changed horses three times, at solitary round white glaring ovens; and were not sorry when we got to Moses' Well to find our Egyptian cavalry escort waiting for us. At the same time we overtook the mail, which had started while we were at dinner, on, I should think, a hundred camels. These last three miles into Suez were enjoyable enough. The road was more level: we felt secure; and the bright Oriental appearance of our caravan was as picturesque as tawdry dirt could make it.

On arriving at Suez, a miserable little Egyptian steamer took us at once from the wharf to the *Bentinck*, lying nearly three miles off, outside the sand-spits, which M. de Lesseps says he can get rid of. Getting on board the *Bentinck*, we at once found we were "on the other side"—as the tracks are called between Suez and China. There were heavy punkahs swinging over the tables. The candles had glass shades to them; strange insects were lying drowned in the oil of the cabin lamps; and the crew were composed of Lascars, Sepoys, Cin-galese, Malays, "Simale-boys," "Seedy-boys," Ethiopians (firemen), and Chinese. The latter were, out and away, the cleanest and most indus-trious. The row these creatures made, when the mails and baggage were being embarked—the native swearing, chattering, fighting, and jabbering—was awful, and prevented anything like sleep all night.

Monday, 19th.—The terrible heat of the Red Sea is making itself felt. I began to register it, from a little thermometer in my cabin, which was forward, and consequently a little cooler than the aft-saloons. This morning at ten it is 91°. * Went to sleep after breakfast on the saloon skylight, and slept till one P.M., during which time we had started. Found a great difference in the dinners on this side. The poultry was so ludicrously small and thin, that we called the chickens "clippers," from their sharp bows; the mutton, too, was tough and poor; the eggs about the size of pigeons'; and the curry, to speak mildly, suspicious. I got very tired of this constantly-recurring, scrap-concealing mess. I have a horrid recollection of having one day detected the same peculiarly-shaped bone on the occasion of its third appearance. The claret and the madeira—also the pale ale—were excellent, and *à discrétion.* The port was what port might be expected to be, when kept on an eternal joggle. The soda-water from Calcutta was tepid and execrable, and now and then of a light straw-colour. I must add, there was an extreme liberality in the supply of everything; but the things were bad in themselves. The punkahs were at work all dinner time, and blew the dishes cold, almost as soon as they were on the table.

The shores of the Red Sea are irregular burnt-up tawny hills, without a trace of animal or vegetable life. The passengers and crew slept about the two decks all day long; the natives, especially, lay about the main deck in all directions, so that it took some care to avoid treading on them, when you went to your cabin. They had all a most marvellous property of sitting on their haunches, like monkeys, to work; and they pared potatoes, encircling their legs with their hands, in a very odd fashion. Bored to bed at 9.30.

Tuesday, 20th (91°).—Found out that the fore-part of the boat was four or five degrees cooler than the quarter deck. The crew were all busy. The Chinese carpenter held a bit of wood he was planing by his foot, as a parrot would do. They brought out the Brahmin cows to be washed: and then sluiced, and scraped, and swabbed the decks, according to the uncomfortable wont of sailors, until there was not a dry place left to sit upon. The monotony of a sea voyage is awful; almost as bad as being shut up with a fool in a yacht, or yatch, or however it is spelt, for I never recollect, so I'll call it a "yot." Once I knew a fool who kept a "yot," not because he liked it, for it made him sick, but because it was "the sort of thing to do." I give my honour that, passing a day with him, the only excitement (as I do not smoke, and could not drink unceasingly from after breakfast until bed-time), was lowering a boat, getting four men into it, and then pulling off to the town for some mutton-chops! At night we slept in long boxes with the fronts knocked out, put on shelves. And there were noble hotels, within a good stone's throw, wherein we might have dined and slept like kings. But that was *not* the thing to do.

The French *gazogènes* in the Peninsular and Oriental boats would be

---

* The degree of heat is taken according to Fahrenheit's scale. It will be mentioned all along the Red Sea. It is understood that this is taken in the shade of the cabin in the morning, and it will be indicated thus: (91°).

a great success; for then people would only take as much ærated
water as they wanted, instead of wasting an entire bottle.
Wednesday, 21st (92°).—On looking out of my port this morning,
about five o'clock, I saw the sun rising blood red, over the Asiatic
coast, and the sea perfectly calm, like an expanse of blue glass. I was
literally streaming with perspiration, and my pillow was quite wet
from my forehead. All the passengers complaining more or less—very
seedy, and unable to eat. Dozed through the greater part of the day.
Thursday, 22nd (93°).—Heat increasing, and did not sleep more
than a quarter of an hour at a time all night long. The people are
lying about perfectly helpless, and gasping like fish on the floor of a punt.
We had despatches for H.M.S. *Cyclops*, and we arrived off Djedda,
the seat of the late Christian massacre, about 10 A.M. The town
appeared to run up from the sea, like a very little Algiers. Some
Arab feluccas were at anchor, off the port, with twenty large sailing
ships and one paddle-steamer, for bringing the pilgrims back from
Mecca, all with Turkish and Egyptian flags. The armoury of the *Bentinck* had been surveyed in the morning. It was not a brilliant one. The
swords had edges as blunt as silver dessert-knives, and one pistol had
a lock, the hammer of which was cocked back with a bit of string
which had to be cut before it went off. Two cannon were run out,
and there appeared to be a difference of opinion as to how they ought
to be loaded. Presently a little sailing boat, with two men in it, put
off from Djedda, and came towards us. One man got on board and
said he was the pilot. The Rev. Mr. Badger, of Aden, who speaks the
Arab dialects fluently, took him into the captain's cabin, and interro-
gated him. He said that the *Cyclops* had not returned yet, that no
Bedouin boats had left Djedda, and that the place was now tranquil.
And indeed well it might be, for they had murdered every Christian.
This man was in a dreadful fright all the time he was on board; but
we bought a fish of him, and gave him a bottle of rum and some beef;
and we parted with a hundred salaams. As we left, the Mohammedan
ships fired off their guns, it being a religious festival day: we fired
ours; and so ended what we called "The Battle of Djedda." "Bentinck Square" is where the officers of the ship live on the lower deck,
breathing from a windsail. Mr. Smith, the first officer, had a piano in
his cabin, so we got up a small concert to-night, and drank much
"soda and sherry." The cabins were fitted up according to their
tastes. One officer had daguerrotypes of all his family, and his little
country home in Devonshire; another inclined to pretty girls' heads;
and another to religious works only. It was so hot that nearly everybody slept on deck to-night. I got the top of the saloon skylight, and
in the night nearly tumbled down through the hole of the windsail.
Mr. Purves, of Singapore, lent me a long pad, upon which I slept, on
and off, until four, when the old nuisance of washing the decks chivied
us all away.
Friday, 23rd (93°).—There was a brisk wind this morning, which
quite blew about my things in the cabin, but it appeared doubly hot
after, and the butcher was struck by the sun. Had a lesson on the
sextant, and was told at 11 A.M. that we were then going under the
sun, and would soon leave him to the north. The heat increased terribly with the day, nevertheless. We lost a good deal of time by

sounding what was thought to be a shoal, but which turned out to be without any fathomable bottom. Nobody ate much dinner, but drank everything they could get, although the liquids were all as warm as the air. *Saturday, 24th* (97°).—Our hottest day :* it broke warm and damp with a cloudy sky. I felt my wet forehead in the night, as if it were covered with minute grains, and on getting up found the " prickly heat " full out all over me, like incipient measles. Everybody said it was very healthy, and the best thing that could happen, but I hated it; it was something between pins and needles, and nettlerash. Went down to Bentinck-square to see Mr. Smith, who was not well; and had my first lesson in " Pigeon English " from the Chinese carpenter. To bed on the skylight, as usual, but the heat was terrific. I could not sleep, but sat upright, half stupified, not knowing what to do. About three in the morning a sudden and very violent storm of rain came on, which lasted ten minutes, but it did not clear the hot air much, only turning it into hot vapour.

Sunday, 25th (89°).— Out of the Straits of Bab-el-Mandeb, and experienced at once a difference for the better in the temperature. At 9 we sighted Aden, and arrived there early in the afternoon, having attended church in the saloon, where Mr. Badger preached the most excellent and practical sermon I ever heard. Not a soul was bored by it. Went on board the *Azov*, which was to take some of our passengers down to the Mauritius and then to shore, in a boat rowed by nearly naked men, who had daubed their heads with red clay. Aden has been compared by wicked men, to " H—— with the fire gone out." It is a glowing calcined succession of peaks and plains without the slightest vegetation. Rode to the cantonments and town, which are about three miles from the port. The town has the appearance of being built in the crater of an extinct volcano. There are long one-storied rows of shops, kept by Parsees—such as Cursedjee Dirtyjee Jabberjehoy, and Lalleballoo Tol Lol—with verandahs in front, and attempts to make little india-rubber plants grow. Down by the shore had formerly been an hotel, kept also by Parsees, but it was now done up—they said so many people ran away without paying them, but by the look of it, it was evidently a bad thing. On board the *Azov* again, to wish our old fellow-travellers God speed, and then to the *Bentinck*.

Monday, 26th (85°).— Went on shore with Captain Curling, to breakfast with Mr. Thomas, the P. and O. agent at Aden, who lives on the top of a hill, in a nice bungalow, all made of cane and matting—and something between a basket and a bird-cage. Nothing could exceed the hospitality of our kind host and hostess, and the change from the steamer was most agreeable. After breakfast, Mr. Thomas lent us his buggy, in which Captain Curling and I set off on an exploring expedition.

Everybody going on shore at Aden should pay a visit to the tanks. There is no water here, and many ages ago huge excavations were made, near the town, to collect the rain water from the mountains—*when* it rains : about once in three years. They are now repairing and closing up these old tanks with cement in the clefts, as well as build-

---

* In the steamer that followed us with the next mail, a lady died from the heat at this part of the Red Sea, off Djebel Tor.

ing an extraordinary arrangement of bridges, platforms, walls, and channels to direct the courses of the water. The poor devils at work carried the stones on the top of their heads, and had fellows to keep them to it with whips. The ground was so intensely hot, that we could not stand long in one place. I question whether these tanks will eventually answer, as the cement was made with sea-water, and appeared to hold but badly. Mr. Thomas has, however, set up a condensing apparatus near the port, which will yield an unlimited supply of water. Cool drinks awaited our return to the bungalow, and I saw the most extraordinary parrot to talk that I ever conceived possible. He spoke English and Hindostanee, and when the purser of the *Bentinck*, Mr. Hatchet, came in, he said, "That boy will be the death of me; he is so jolly green!" and then went off into fits of laughter. We had an excellent little roast pig for dinner. In the evening I had another drive, with Mr. Thomas; and then on board to sign the "coal warrants," which means to have a parting drink. Just as we were leaving, at 7 P.M., our hawser broke, and the ship swung round, so we had to wait until the next tide.

Tuesday, 27th (87°).—At 3 A.M. they began to try and get the *Bentinck* off, with no end of bawling and countermanding, and she was floating at daybreak. Previously the night had been very lovely, with a full moon:

> "All night the splinter'd crags that wall'd the dell,
> With spires of silver shone."

The wind rose as we got out, and the boat began to labour, which was rather a good thing, as it kept some of the incessant talkers quiet, and some more did not show at dinner. Obliged to wade through the coal water that floated the main deck to my cabin, where I slept, as the ship was altogether in a dirty mess. Although the port was wide open, and the wind blowing in, I was almost suffocated.

Wednesday, 28th (96°).—Another regular Red Sea "blazer," and the "prickly heat" running riot and stinging me almost beyond endurance; otherwise in good condition. The *Bentinck* labouring heavily in the S.W. monsoon.

I was writing in the saloon about 1.30 P.M., when I heard a loud bang, accompanied by a shock which sent everything off the table. My first impression was that the ship had struck on a rock. Everybody rushed on deck, the stewardess crying out, "My God, she's gone!" I followed them, and found the deck enveloped in steam, which was pouring up from all the hatchways, and all the people running about and screaming. Mrs. H. and Miss L. came to me carrying the children, in a terrible way, begging I would tell them what was the matter. We all expected we were going down. After a little while, Mr. Hope—our able and intelligent engineer (not at all, it must be understood, resembling my old friend Edwards, of the Austrian Lloyd's)—went down with one or two of his "subs," and the anxiety was very great. We soon heard that one of the cylinders of the engine had burst, from the lower beam giving way. A consultation was held as to what must be done. Some said we must go back to Aden and wait for the next mail, which would have been very cheerful; others that we must proceed under sail, and that the old *Bentinck* would not do above three knots an hour, which would make a

month to Ceylon. At last, Mr. Hope having ordered and superin-
tended a great deal of timbering up and unscrewing, told me we could
perhaps go on with one engine. At dinner we all sat down pretty
quiet and cross, but just before dessert we were rejoiced to feel the
paddles vibrate again.

It had been so stifling in the cabin last night that I took up my old
quarters on the skylight, and Mr. Catton, a young surgeon going to
India, occupied the bench under me. About midnight the *Bentinck*
gave a lurch, and shot us both off—bedding and all—down upon the
deck; so I took the hint and went below. I never passed such a
wretched night. The sea rose tremendously, and I was shaken from
one side of my berth to the other, until I got actually sore; with
a constant fear of falling off, and my sheet getting all into a ruck, and
leaving only the horsehair for me to lie upon, which was worse than
the prickly heat. I did not sleep a wink, for, added to this, the sea
made a great noise, and the bulkheads were creaking and separating
all round the cabin. "She did *worrick* dreadful," as the quarter-
master said next day; "and I wouldn't a been on the sponsons for
nothink." Towards morning I got into another berth, where I was at
right angles to the roll of the boat, and here I slept a little, but very
little, as the Jackos (so we called the native crew) began all the noise
and chattering again.

Thursday, 29th (86°).—Got up at seven, very worn and tired, and
dressing, in the rolling of the ship, with great difficulty. Scarcely
anybody on deck—the wind and the sea keeping it up between them,
and everything wet and miserable. The "fiddles" (frames of wood
tied to the table, to keep things in their places) were used at breakfast, and the crockery kept leaping about and smashing in a very
uncomfortable manner. I got up to the stern of the saloon after
breakfast, but it was too rough to write, and I was too tired to
read, and not tired enough to go to sleep, so I rolled about and half
dozed, and was very blinky and stupid; but it got certainly much
cooler, for we had no awning, and the sky was one uniform
grey. Did not care much for dinner, and the things were not very
appetizing in themselves. The wind and sea fell as we got under
the lee of Socotra, and then the passengers' spirits rose in proportion.
Some of them played vingt-un, with nuts for counters; and, of course,
the cadets going out, who could least afford it, lost. These poor boys
should not be allowed to play. The instant I heard one especial
"party" cry "double all round," I knew they were done. Our usual
little knot together for grog at "one bell first watch" (which means
half-past eight—much more sensible), including Captain Maguire, of
H.M.S. *Sanspareil*; Captain Clark, of the Mysore Commission; young
Elliott, going out to join; and Mr. Fisher, in Jardine's house, at Hong Kong.

Friday, 30th (78°).—A rolling stormy night, and the sea high in the
morning. The Monsoon "going it." All the boats are lashed, by
ropes across the deck, so that you have to bob under them when you
walk along, as on a racecourse. The people are all huddled about
wherever they can get in the dry. The tossing worse than yesterday.
Got bored upon deck, and went to my cabin; got bored there, and
came upon deck again, and wished I was anywhere else.

At dinner everything was lashed again, but the sea was running so high, that just as we were sitting down, all the soup flew at Dr. Little, and covered him. Then a pigeon pie shot at the Punkah-puller's head, and then our seat broke from the floor with a lurch, and three of us threw a back somerset. After dinner the gamblers struggled at vingt-un again, but with great difficulty.

I come down to tea every night simply because it is *something to do;* but it only makes me hot and fidgetty afterwards. I am really getting terribly bored—have read all my books—cannot make up my mind to write, and am only thinking of home.

Saturday 31*st* (from this point to China the thermometer varied between 80° and 90°).—Having again suffered considerably from the heat, which the ship's thermometer did not justify, I found that it had been wafted into my cabin from the engine-room, the forge, the oven, and the cooking, all combined, with the various attendant smells. The sea has somewhat gone down.

Sunday, August 1*st.*—A good night's rest—indeed I did not awake until the breakfast-bell rung. A good wind and all sails set. Church at half-past ten. We had another parson to-day—not a bad fellow at all ; but his voice was scarcely loud enough for the saloon, and I did not hear his sermon very well, as the wind made a noise. But, from what I could gather, it recommended us to control our desires. Hoped F. would benefit by it, as he always took too much preserved ginger— the young and tender shoots too—at dessert. About eight P.M. it got very cloudy, and the captain had the topsails taken down, or in, or whatever they call it. A very nice lady of our party, whose husband was with his ship at Calcutta, said the captain would "furl the wind-sails next." This made great fun—but it must be remembered we were on board ship.

Monday, 2*nd.*—The Jackos began their row about four this morning: and soon came unholy smells of tobacco, and onions, and burnt *ghee* (most offensive), and Ess : Blacky, and foul things generally. Mr. Ray, the Government agent, is a very nice old gentleman. He amuses himself with water-colour drawing : and has excellent sketches of Aden, Singapore, the wreck of the *Douro*, &c. Two terrible children worry him much, and mess his paints when he is not looking: they are of the real offensive "sharp-little-things" school, with large eyes and gappy teeth.

This evening we played Sea-Quoits on deck. The quoits are made of pieces of rope spliced into rings, and we chalk a scheme upon deck, thus:—

B		
50	100	70
80	40	60
20	10	30

The game is 300, and is played like hopscotch. Quoits pitched on the line don't count, and if you go into B, you lose altogether; and as many as you get *above* 300 is subtracted from your score. The boys again lost more than they could afford, and a man, whom I did not think a great deal of during the voyage, generally won their money.

Tuesday, 3rd.—Rather hot again, the pillow feeling warmer than my head. Went into Mr. Hope's cabin and saw the drawings he has made of the accident to the engine. He says he could take her home round the Caps, now, by hooping up the broken cylinder. Borrowed "Digby Grand" of him, and read it, but was disappointed. It is a succession of detached descriptive scenes, and no characters—the plot seems a mere thread on which to hang a lot of *tableaux*. It is astonishing how hard everything you sit on, on board ship, gradually becomes. Slept on deck again. About one, four large spots of rain fell, and no more.

Wednesday, 4th.—At luncheon—the people call it "tiffin," but I don't see the necessity—we have little dice of damp cheese, which are, as people say in a great state of sudden alarm, "all in a cold sweat." It is a pity the punkah makes everything so cold at dinner. If they would only ice the drinks instead of the hashed mutton, what an improvement it would be! To-day we had a raffle in Mr. Smith's cabin for a revolver—twenty one members at eight rupees (sixteen shillings). I threw thirty-seven, the winner thirty-nine. Hate raffles. It rained heavily at night, and this drove all the Jackos down to the hot main deck in their soaked clothes, which they never take off. In consequence, the atmosphere around and in my cabin was not nice.

Thursday, 5th.—Bright hot morning, and the sea very calm. The morning passed pleasantly with Kingsley's "Two years ago," which is a charming story. All the passengers have got so worn out with the prolongation and monotony of the voyage that they would quarrel for a relief, if anybody would start a row. After dinner the parson showed us a curious revolving and self-sustaining instrument, called a Gyroscope. A disturbance to-night amongst the Vingt-un party, about a shilling put on, or not put on, or doubled, or something, which got to a pitch really amusing. I had almost suspected that this would come.

Friday, 6th.—This day a fight took place between one of the P. and O. officers on board—not belonging to our ship—and one of the Chinamen; so they put the Chinaman in irons, somewhere below Bentinck-square, where he looked dull enough.

Saturday, 7th.—At daybreak we were in sight of Ceylon, and we steamed very cautiously up to Galle, and into a small bay edged with cocoa-nuts, palms, and other lovely specimens of tropical vegetation. It was very pleasant to see leaves again, after the all but calcined land we had passed. The first thing that astonished me was the pilot's canoe, which was very long and very narrow—not more than eighteen inches broad—and with its seven or eight occupants, looking like a gigantic pea-shuck, with the peas putting their heads out of it. They had an enormous outrigger of timber, in shape like a shuttle, and twelve or fourteen feet long, lashed to the port-side of the boat, about seven feet away from it; so that it was impossible to upset it.

We had great fun with some of the ladies, who would try these frail boats, even with crinoline : the results were terrible. On shore, to the P. and O. office, held in a picturesque old Dutch gateway, with a fine bread-fruit tree in front of it. Met Captain Bayley there, with Mr. Sparkes, the agent, an old Merchant-Taylor, who showed me every attention, from cool beer upwards. Afterwards walked with Captain Bayley round the ramparts and towns. The houses have porticos like those at Aden, and there are screens in the open doorways to maintain the privacy of the interiors, with neat light cane blinds everywhere. At a Parsee jeweller's I saw some pretty work in porcupine quills and white tortoise-shell; also two of my own books for sale— "Ledbury" and "Christopher Tadpole," which had a familiar look six thousand miles from home. From the ramparts, a portion of the shore reminded me very much of Capri. Vast piles of coral were lying about, used for building, and cocoa nuts and plantains were everywhere, close down to the sea ; the ground was also cumbered with stone blocks, for a lighthouse, to be put up some day. There is a smaller one, on one of the points, which I at once remembered to have seen in London, when it was put up for a day or two, the other side of the water.

Back to chat at the office. The clerks are Parsees, and appear very attentive and industrious. I saw here, by the China papers, that the cholera was raging at Hong Kong. There had been a concert last night in Galle, supported by the passengers of the *Emu*, now in the harbour from Australia. They had only two performers—a Mossoo who fiddled, and an amateur who accompanied him. The concert was for the benefit of Mossoo, because he had been so festive during the voyage. Wandered about for an hour or two by myself—first into a green square surrounded by trees, with a well of good water in the middle. The people drove about in little four-wheeled carriages, called *garries*—very open and airy, and well made. The men are very nearly naked. They wear combs, twist up their back-hair into a knot, and sit on their haunches with marvellous flexibility. Then to the water-side outside the gate, to sit on a stone under the bread-fruit tree, and watch the people coming and going. They offered walking sticks for sale, with models of the canoes, and rulers of black wood. They also sold cocoa nuts, plantains, and betel nuts. Most of them carried Chinese umbrellas, and it was excessively difficult to tell the men from the women.

At 3, wished them good bye on board the old *Bentinck*, and then to the *Norna*, for the China line, in a canoe, the men of which ate cocoa nut and then drank salt water. It was never terrifically hot, all day, but an English dog-day's temperature. Sharks abound all round Galle, but never come into the harbour, so the fellows bathe there.

The China passengers gradually came on board the *Norna*—eight or ten only. I bought some green (ripe) oranges, and some pomelos— red inside and not very juicy. Covent Garden against the world, for everything.

We had a very good dinner, with Shanghae mutton. The *cuisine* was a grand step in advance of the *Bentinck*. Captain Rogers is an excellent fellow, and knows well what he is about ; and his nice wife, who accompanied him on the voyage, made everything bright and agreeable.

After dinner the mails and luggage came on board. The natives worked
very hard, and shining with perspiration looked like fine bronze statues.
They waited until the luggage-boat rose with the heavy swell to a level
with the sponsons, and then heaved the box on board. It is astonishing
that scarcely anything is ever lost. At last we got everything on board,
and should have done so much sooner, but for the delay of the *Bentinck*—who could not get out that night, Galle harbour being very
intricate and dangerous—so blew off her steam about half-past six.
About seven the *Norna* started, burning blue lights, and the anchor
coming up to a fiddle and fife playing "The King of the Cannibal
Islands." Boats had been sent out with torches to the dangerous
rocks, and the general effect was very pretty. Like most narrow
screws, the *Norna* rolls very much; and we had the "fiddles" again
at dinner. Walked up and down the deck with Captain Maguire
until tired, and then to bed. A very good day.

Sunday, 8th.—The ship's company mustered at half-past ten, and
looked very clean and bright in their gay colours. After that, Captain
Rogers read the service. The *Norna* rolled on with a spanking
breeze, at twelve knots an hour. After dinner we drank "Absent
friends." There were two Mahommedans with us, who dined by
themselves afterwards. There were knives and forks placed for them,
but they ate everything with their fingers, with large round soft cakes,
like crumpets, for their plates. Our dessert consisted of plantains,
pines, and pomelos.

Monday 9th.—We are now in the middle of the Bay of Bengal ; and
the sea and the screw together make the boat vibrate so, that it is
almost impossible to write. But, notwithstanding the high sea and
the rolling, we are making capital way. In the afternoon they shut
up the ports on the weather side, which at once brought the temperature of my cabin up to 88°, so I determined to sleep on deck. I
brought up my two pillows, and Mr. Morel, the Admiralty agent,
exchanged his blanket for my counterpane, and I made up my bed on
the saloon skylight, together with Major Mein, of the 1st Royals,
until a shower drove him below. I did not make much of a sleep of
it, as the *Norna* lurched so, I was obliged to hold on with my hands to
keep from slipping down. At last, about one, the ship gave such a roll
that I was shot off; so I moved all my traps down upon the deck close
under the skylight, but there was no awning here, and the wind blew
terribly. I then moved to the lee of the compass, and slept until they
came to clean the decks, which forced me below ; but the heat of the
cabin was so awful I laid down on one of the saloon seats, from which
I was soon rolled off. I next contrived to beat open the port in my
cabin, but a heavy sea came in and I was compelled to close it again.
I hitched the door open as far as the hook would go, and was then in
a perspiration that I could run off my chest and temples with my
fingers. A large rat came out of Mr. Hill's, the purser's, cabin, but I
threw a shoe at him and he went away. About half-past five, Carolus,
the steward, came in and opened the port, when the wind came in well,
and I directly went off to sleep.

Tuesday, 10th.—The weather greatly improved, and the ports open
all over the ship. Some of the people say that the smell of the opium
cargo, which is very strong, makes them drowsy. I was very drowsy

myself, with my uncomfortable night, so I turned in after breakfast
and slept well till noon. The other passengers did not read, or do
anything; they would sit for hours looking at the sea, or trimming
their nails with penknives, or talking mercantile, about freights, and
exchanges, and dollars. Many had lived years in China, but could
tell me absolutely nothing about it. Their minds had become reduced
to what they worked in—the "godowns" or stores. Two lady passengers made a noise because they did not have sausages enough for
breakfast; and the stewardess—a gaunt, tall, masculine woman,
generally termed "the Old Duke"—could not appease them. I did
not like this stewardess. She had a terrible temper, but put on an
equally terrible smile when she spoke to the children, if their parents
were near. Had tea on deck with Mr. Fleetwood, the engineer, who
told me more things I wanted to know about China, in ten minutes,
than all the "tea-tasters" put together during the voyage. At night
felt one or two things creep over me—I expect cockroaches.

Wednesday, 11*th*.—A calm bright morning, with little or no sea,
and light fleecy clouds. We are now in the Straits of Malacca, and
can see the Gold Mountain (10,000 feet) in Sumatra, on our right, like
a cone on the horizon. The Jackos are cleaning the arms. Captain
Rogers tells me they keep on at work for hours, as long as they can
squat down at it; but they hate being on their legs, and their severest
punishment is to be made to walk up and down, with a knapsack. All
the passengers are getting uncommonly idle and sleepy in the middle
of the day. Some burrow in their cabins, and appear to be insensible
of the heat. Finished a letter home, to post to-morrow at Penang.
Slept on deck, and very well too.

Thursday, 12.—When we came on deck this morning Penang was
on our right, with irregular hills covered with jungle, and little bays
and beaches, looking very green and pleasant. About nine, I saw a
real Chinese junk under sail ; and an hour after we came in sight of
Penang, with many ships in the harbour. Dropped anchor about
noon, and went on shore in a boat with Mr. Padday, who had been my
companion all the way from London. We went to breakfast with him
in his bungalow, in a little rattling *garry*—it is called a *palky* here—
which appeared to be made of matting and bandbox. The bungalow
was pleasantly situated, almost on the beach, with a nice wind blowing
through the jalousies, and surrounded by a pretty garden of
tropical plants, with an approach of plantains and palms. We first
drove to the cascade, along admirable roads, with a suburban sea-side
watering-place look about the villas. The streets had English
names, such as Light-street, Love-lane, Old Battery Street, &c., &c. I
also noticed "Dr. Scott" on a board. There was a neat church, and
some dissenting edifices, and little Chinese shed-shops, with their
names and trades in black letters on red grounds. Some had betel-nut
plantations attached to them, and in all the gardens were cocoa-nuts
and plantains. The road stops suddenly at the gate of a nutmeg plantation, leading to the cascade, which reminded me of the Mortlake
entrance to Richmond Park. There was a shed for the horses on the
right, under a very fine tree. Here we found Captain and Mrs.
Rogers, who had shot past us on the road in a *palky*, drawn
by the smallest and best piebald pony I ever saw. We all went on

B

together through the nutmeg thicket; and at the lower pool of the waterfall met Major Mein and Captain Maguire, who had been taking a bath. What a luxury the fresh sparkling water was! Then I went on with Mr. Padday to the very top of the fall—the others shirking. The path was very steep, and over decomposed granite, very like the top of the Col de Colma, between Orta and Varallo. There were lovely ferns, sensitive plants, and rhododendrons, all the way. The cascade is as pretty as any of the second-rank falls in Switzerland, and has several leaps. When we returned to the shed, we found Captain Rogers with a cool bottle of champagne, which we shared. We also bought dozens of *mangosteens* on our way home. The fruit is about the size of an average apple, with a thick tough red rind or coat. On breaking this in half you find the fruit—the bigness of a Tangerine orange, and like it, in quarters, but quite white, and almost as cold as ice. It could be well imitated with vanille and lemon cream. We also bought other fruits, of new and strange species. One, the *rambutan*, was like a scarlet horse-chesnut, which opened on a pulp resembling a boiled plover egg, with the stone for the yolk; the other, the name of which I forget, resembled a small white turnip-radish, with a transparent pulp also. Mr. Padday took us to his godown, and gave us some "Penang lawyers," and a large basket of fruit; and then, with many thanks and good wishes, we went back to the *Norna*.

There was an execution yesterday at Penang—the sufferer was the first white man ever hung there. He was a seaman on board an American ship—the *Golden State*—and was hung for mutiny and murder of the mate. The wife of the captain, a pleasant little American lady, here joined us, accompanied by Mr. Biddles, the American consul at Singapore. Towards night, the ladies who complained about the sausages kicked up a terrible shine about a black maid, who had been put in their cabin to tea. They dived down into their cabins—then shot up again—then down once more, pouring out volleys of abuse upon everybody each time, for we were all roaring with laughter; and with this the evening passed well. A very sultry night, with no wind, when we started. Slept on deck, on a fine couch of coiled ropes, until five in the morning, when a vivid storm, with rain and lightning, drove me below.

Friday, 13*th.*—A dead calm this morning, and the sea with a quietly undulating surface, calm enough to reflect the clouds. Passed a fixed light here, in a boat, under which, in the middle of the Strait, there is only six feet of water. Whilst I was writing, the "Old Duke" and the negro maid came to lunch near me, and they had a long inconsecutive argument about slavery, the stewardess saying there were no slaves in America who had to clean London doorsteps in cold winter mornings; and this clencher settled the question. At night we got up a small miscellaneous entertainment, which went off pleasantly; but little matters please on board ship. Mr. Biddles had a bottle of "cock-tail" with him, which he said no Yankee ever travelled without, and very good it was. Slept on the skylight, by Captain Rogers, who was on deck all night, the navigation being somewhat ticklish here. Came down at deck-washing time, and found the rats had carried away the tongues of my lace-up shoes, and the cockroaches had eaten all the bindings.

Saturday, 14*th.*—Land in sight from the time of getting up. Dropped anchor in Singapore roads at 10.30, and on shore with one of the passengers, getting a large bed-room between us, at the Hotel de l'Esperance, on the Esplanade, at Singapore. Went, first of all, to Captain Marshall, the P. and O. agent, who was very polite, and told me I must know Mr. Whampoa—a leading China merchant, living close by. He sent me round, with a clerk, and a very valuable introduction it proved to me. I found Whampoa—as he is universally called—sitting at his warehouse door, watching his boat unlading. He spoke English perfectly, and received me with excellent English courtesy. After a little talk he dispatched me, with one of his men, to see the Buddhist Temples, or Joss Houses, in the town. They are very striking to a stranger, and elaborate in hideous images, gold, and carving. A man was in one, burning joss-stick, and throwing up two bits of wood, to tell his fortune from the manner in which they fell. Grim figures every where met the eye ; and there were two large tanks, without water, at the bottom of which a few sacred tortoises crawled lazily about. At the gate was a statue of a lion, with a large ball carved in his mouth, which turned round but would not come out. When we had been over the temple, on which was hung an enormous drum and bell—to call the Joss's attention, when they think he is not listening—the priest took a bottle of stout from behind an altar, which I enjoyed very much. I gave him a rupee, and the old boy "chin-chin'd" me to the ground. I saw many other temples, but none so grand as this. Back to Whampoa, who asked me to dine with him that day. I then took my umbrella, and wandered about the town, infinitely amused and interested. The shops are all under porticos, and the houses only a story high—all kept and inhabited by Chinese. Their names and trades were mostly painted in vermilion, and some-times gilt, on black boards, and written perpendicularly. Tailors and barbers are very frequently combined, in the same shop. The tailors sat at tables covered with fine matting, and the barbers' strops were very long and hung from the ceiling. They shaved without lather, but with rice-water, and then shampoo'd their customers, and with many litttle instruments cleaned their eyes and ears. Scribes sat gravely at tables under the porticos. One was doing a book. It was on very thin paper, and under this he placed a guide, so that the characters showed through. These he traced, working very quickly. Another was a grey-headed old man, like an owl, with a white beard and whiskers, and wearing enormous pantomime spectacles. He was adding ver-milion dots and rings, here and there, to the pages already done. Over the doorways fluttered little labels of red paper, gilt and perforated, put there on New Year's day. In the carpenters' shops the planes had a handle on each side; and one man was doing some work, and at the same time rolling a grindstone backwards and forwards with his feet over some blue powder in a concave trough. In front of some of the houses were curious representations of birds, animals, and flowers, made of broken crockery, let into the cement. I also saw a walking *restaurateur*. His 'establishment' consisted of two square stands, with little rails three parts round the top. In one was a fire-place, and small copper, with a stove of fuel underneath. On the top of the other, in little bowls, were his chief articles of food—oysters, picked shrimps, onions, a sort of maccaroni, and scraps of meat and duck. Underneath these were drawers with more things in them. While there, a customer ate a little basin of soup with oysters in it, with a horn spoon. It all looked very clean, and appeared an excellent thing. When no customer came the man knocked two bits of bamboo together, to attract attention.

At half-past four I went back to Whampoa, and sat and talked with him at the door, whilst the people came up offering ducks and poultry for sale, as well as canes and walking-sticks. In the street they sold bits of sugar cane, about nine inches long, to the boys, with slices of pine-apple, for the smallest possible coin. Paid a visit to Mr. Woods, of the *Straits Times*—an important paper out here. His compositors were all foreigners, and he showed me his different presses, chiefly American. One small hand one, by Orcutt, of Boston, was one of the cleverest things I ever saw for simple rapidity. Captain Maguire now joined me, and we went off to Whampoa's in his carriage.

He first took us to his country house, now uninhabited. It was the perfect residence of a Chinese gentleman. There was a very large garden with bamboo hedges and large fish tanks, edged with walls of blue bricks and perforated tiles. His pigs were in admirable condition, and as beautifully kept as the Prince Consort's at Windsor. About the grounds were nutmegs, mangosteens, plantains, cocoa-nuts, dariens, and small creepers, trained into baskets and pagodas. Inside the house the drawing-rooms had doors sliding across circular openings. We then went on to this good gentleman's private residence, entering by a Chinese triumphal gate. He tells me he has ten miles of carriage road round his estate. It is on a fine undulating tract of land, reclaimed from the jungle, and laid out with rare taste. In the outskirts a tiger killed a man the other day. In his garden I found Jacko, living in a cane cage, next door to a porcupine; there were also some rare birds. Further on, some very small Brahmin bulls, a Cashmere goat, and a family of young kangaroos. There were all sorts of unknown beautiful flowers placed about in enormous China vases. Here I first saw the tea-plant growing. It is of the camellia tribe, three or four feet high perhaps, and bears a small white flower, like an open dog-rose. Also I was shown the "moon-flower," a kind of rounded convolvulus that only opens at night. There was a bower of "monkey-cups"—the pitcher-flower, which collects water, and from which Jacko refreshes himself in the jungles. The fan palm—a beautiful tree on the lawn—produced water by being pierced with a penknife, of clear cold quality. Several minute creepers were trained over wire forms, to imitate dragons, with egg shells for their eyes ; and there were many of the celebrated dwarf trees—the first I had seen—little oaks and elms about eighteen inches high, like small withered old men. The house, here, was superbly furnished in the English style, but with lanterns all about it. At six the guests arrived — mostly English — including Captain Marshall, and all dressed in short white jackets and trousers. The dinner was admirably served, in good London style, and all the appointments as regarded plate, glass, wines, and dishes, perfect. The quiet, attentive waiting of the little China boys deserved all praise. After dinner, we lounged through the rooms, decorated with

English prints of the Royal family, statuettes, '*curios*' from every part of the world, and rare objects in jade-stone, and crackle china, also a portrait of our host's son, who is being educated in Edinburgh. He was in English dress.

About nine we all drove down, in various traps, to the theatre. It was an enormous tent, as big as the old Free Trade Hall, at Manchester; and made entirely of bamboos and matting, very light and strong. The people sat round the sides, and the "swells" in the area and pit, in comfortable cane chairs. The stage was lighted by pots of shreds in oil, such as they clean engines with; and the orchestra sat at the back of, and on, it. There was a large Chinese scroll at the back, on which was the name of the theatre. The female characters were played by men, who all sang in a shrill *falsetto*, and the plot was very straggling and obscure. The change of scene was effected by merely taking a chair away, or putting on a screen; and when the musicians were not playing, they had a pipe. All the performers came on on the left side, and went off on the right. In one scene there was a general battle, in which there was as much tumbling as fighting, in the violent style of the Bedouin Arabs; in fact, the actors were all, more or less, acrobats. The comic man performed a trick new to me. He jumped up very high, and, whilst in the air, threw his feet forward and kicked his adversary in the chest, knocking him down. At last Whampoa said, "Now they are married, and its all over," so we left, and he drove me to the hotel. The people had all gone to bed, but I kicked up a native who was lying asleep on the ground before the porch, and he lighted me to my room. The other passenger was already in his bed; and I soon got into mine and fell asleep, very tired. I was not troubled with the mosquitoes, although I did not let down the curtains.

Sunday, 15th.—To breakfast with Captain Marshall, at his bungalow. Passed a burial ground at the side of the hill, with many Chinese tombs; also several hovels, where they sold bits of pineapple, plantains, and dried fish; and houses built on piles, in the low-water mud. Noticed a dram-shop, with a sign "Paddy-Goose, by Madras Bob." Captain Marshall's bungalow is charmingly situated on a hill, overlooking the magnificent harbour and docks, now being built by the Peninsular and Oriental Company. We had some of the best mutton I have tasted out; and a prawn curry was—for curry—a great success. The prawns were as large as cray-fish. To the hotel for lunch; and several of us had some champagne, to drink the health of Mr. Purves, whom we left here. Had a good row about the bill. I have a great affection for hotels generally, and this formed no exception. They wanted to charge me three dollars (12s. 6d.) for my bed and the half of the room. The proprietress, Madame Esperanza, had been, as some said, a baroness; according to others, a lady's maid. We, however, made her take off two-thirds of the bill. On board the *Norna*, at 2 P.M., and started at once. In the night, the cockroaches, or rats, or both, finished the hind part of one of my shoes, and carried one of my slippers clean away.

Monday, 16th.—A rattling storm of rain in the night, but at daybreak the sea was like a mill-pond, and the heat once more intense—as overpowering as on the Red Sea. The boats are being taken in

and lashed, in the event of our getting into a typhoon, as we are now
approaching its regions. Another rain-storm came on about noon,
soaking through the awning, and wetting the deck, but the air was
refreshed by it. Established two chairs and a pillow on deck, and
slept well there till deck-washing. Hung my other shoes on the
hooks, out of the way of the marauders.

Tuesday, 17.—A nice breeze this morning, enough to make the
Norna lurch. Nearly all the people asleep between breakfast and
noon, and nothing else to recount during the day.

I was lying on deck about half-past two in the morning, when I saw
two of the crew go to the weather side and point, and presently afterwards they shut down the skylights. Then there was a great mustering
and to-do, amongst the natives, and Captain Rogers came out of his cabin
and told me there was a storm coming on. They were lowering some
of the sails, when a black cloud advanced towards us, and then it began
in all its violence. The wind burst over us, roaring in a frightful
manner, the sea running in enormous waves, and the ship lurched so
that we thought the water must be coming in at the lee ports. The
pine-apples hung over the boats were first blown away, and then the
gangway steps. It was very awful to see the wild foaming water
below us on the lee as we stood holding on tight to the awning irons.
The lightning was incessant—either in summer flashes on the horizon,
or blazing cracks that almost blinded one, and one black cloud kept
coming on after another with a redoubled storm. One or two of the
passengers came up wildly scared, and wet through, having been
washed out of their berths. The squall lessened a little about three in
the morning, and then it began to rain, so I went below, but did not
sleep at all, the boat was rolling so.

Wednesday, 18th.—The air cleared by the storm, but the swell continues. The passengers drowsy, lopping about, or asleep all day.
The day turned out very fine, and the evening lovely; stars innume-
rable, and a bright clear moon.

Thursday, 19th.—Another fine day, and a talk about arriving on
Saturday. Dead calm at night, and all the sails taken down. Mr.
Fisher, who is our weather-prophet, shows us what he calls a "cock's
eye" round the moon, which he says presages a typhoon. General
expression of disbelief in his power of presaging.

Friday, 20th.—This being our last night on board, we got up an
"entertainment." Mr. Hill arrayed the deck with flags and awnings,
and Mr. Soy, the first officer, was the stage director and conductor
of the orchestra, which consisted of a drum, fife, and fiddle. We
made everybody do something; and it went off with a bang. After
this, we had broiled bones and anchovy toast, and punch, and there
was a tremendous deal of speech-making, and congratulating, and
hurrahing, and we kept very bad hours indeed.

Saturday, 21st.—Whilst dressing in the morning, it got very dark,
and when I came on deck there was nothing but a black mist all about
us. Captain Rogers was looking very anxious, as he could not make
out a bearing anywhere. About 9 a heavy storm of rain came on,
making everthing still more obscure, and we went about, off and on,
in great suspense, until noon, when the rock of Mammichoo appeared
through the mist. We passed several Chinese pirates, in pairs, but

they kept well clear of us. Soon the pointed rocks, known as the " Ass's Ears," appeared ; and then islands broke upon us on all sides, and it was all right. At 2 P.M., passing Green Island, we entered Hong Kong harbour.

In a few minutes, Lieutenant Douglas Walker came on board from the flag-ship, the *Calcutta*, for letters, and was kind enough to offer me a berth until I could determine where I should go; for there are no hotels, properly so called, at Hong Kong. A well-conducted house would make a fortune. Then all the boats of the different merchants swarmed alongside for newspapers, intelligence, &c., and *The Home News*, *The Overland Mail*, and *The Straits Times*, were at a high premium. Mr. J. Darby Gibb, to whom I was introduced, was good enough to go off to the Hong Kong Club, and propose me there. Mr. Maclean, of Jardine's house, seconded me, and I was elected at once. Then Mr. Howe took me and my luggage in his own boat to the landing-place at Pedder's Wharf, and I walked up to the Club, where Mr. Chisholm Anstey was waiting to offer me a room in his house; but now it was not necessary, as there are bed-rooms in the Club. I got a charming bed-room, No. 7, at the north-east corner of the building—large and airy, with a pleasant look-out, commanding the harbour in front, and the church, the Bishop's palace, Sir John Bowring's, Colonel Caine's, and the principal street, at the side. Dined by myself in the Club. Had an odd fish, whose name sounded like *groper*, and a little fowl, with good pale ale. There was very bad attendance, as the native servants had all been recalled by an imperial edict, but the ice, and the room, and the steadiness were agreeable, after so much steamboat living. After dinner went out for a stroll— my first walk in China! The shops were very like, but a little superior to, those at Singapore ; and some were closed by bars of wood, like wild beast cages. I met Captain Maguire in the street, in uniform, now appointed to the *Sanspareil*, accompanied by Captain Brookes, of the *Inflexible*, who took the old miscreant Yeh (*Yep*, as the Chinese call him) up to Calcutta. Then with Mr. Anstey and Captain Twiss, of the Artillery, to an American Bar, where we had some excellent sherry-cobblers. There was also a bowling alley here. To bed, very tired, at ten, rolling about in space, to my great delight.

Sunday, 22nd.—Up at six. Unpacked and shook out all my things, and made up a huge bundle for the washerman. Then started in a bamboo chair, carried by two coolies, to breakfast with Mr. Anstey. It was rather a tough pull for them, up hill, and I was overtaken by Captain Twiss, of the Artillery, about half-way up. Mr. Anstey's bungalow is charmingly situated, high up on the spur of Victoria Peak, with a beautiful view of the harbour and Chinese coast. It is surrounded by a large and pretty garden, a great orna- ment everywhere being a creeping convolvulus that covers every- thing. It has leaves shaped like the Virginian creeper. At breakfast we were joined by Mr. Tudor Davis, the magistrate. After breakfast, a Parsee brought a native to consult Mr. Anstey on a knotty law point, and Captain Twiss and I started for a stroll amongst the joss- houses, shops, and streets. Here I first saw a child of about two years old, in a pigtail, sitting in a gutter making dirt pies; and several

women hobbling about on little feet. Came home, in the noon heat, and
got through a quantity of "home pigeon" for the mail, after which Mr.
Fisher called on me, and we took another walk, during which a small
street boy picked my pocket of my note-book : this, for the time,
distressed me very much. Dined at the Club again, off the same odd
fish and small fowl; and at nine went up, with Mr. Anstey (who
carried a handspike against marauders, and has a sharp dog, called
"Tarn"), to call on Mr. Gibb. Found four of his clerks at dinner, in
good style, with a punkah working over them, red pith wine-coolers,
claret, madeira, and an excellent dessert. Walking home Mr. Anstey
suggested that I should call at the Police-office and mention my loss
of the note-book. Met a brother of Mr. May, of Scotland-yard, who
is in office here. He took down the particulars, and I offered a
reward of three dollars for its recovery.

Monday, 23rd.—At half-past six this morning, a note came from
Mr. May, with my note-book, which they had found in a pawn-shop.
This was quick good work. Then, in a chair, to the Magistracy,
where I found Mr. Tudor Davies on the bench, with a sharp young
Portuguese, named Rozario, for an interpreter. It was a good scene.
The Chinese public in general stood about, as at Bow-street; with
several women with small feet, and tanka (or boat) girls, with handkerchiefs tied somewhat coquettishly over their heads. Some of these
were really pretty. I heard two or three cases whilst here. In one,
Hyatt, a publican, summoned his servant A-took for running away
from him. He had evidently been bought over by an opposition inn.
Hyatt did not want him back again, and A-took was in his new place;
so the bench would not allow A-took anything, although he had served
Hyatt three weeks out of four. Then there came on a troublesome case
about selling a ball of opium. A swore that he ordered the ball of B, and
paid for it, but that it was never sent home. B swore it was ; and
called C and D—his shopmen—to prove this. The books were also
produced. B was a known respectable shopkeeper, so A was fined
five dollars for telling lies and taking up the Queen's time. Then
came a case between a Parsee and a Portuguese, about losing a borrowed book. The verdict was, that if Parsee didn't find the book
by Thursday, he was to pay five dollars. I was struck with the
quick perception of Mr. Davies in these matters. He said sometimes it was a very difficult matter to decide, with terribly hard
swearing on each side ; for they had no notion of an oath, and said
anything that suited them. They do not kiss the book, but burn a
bit of yellow paper. I was next introduced to another magistrate,
Mr. Mitchell, in the next court. A new clerk now came as interpreter—an intelligent young Chinaman, in a long white gown, brought
up by one of the missions. He spoke English fluently. The first case
was an assault. Lun, a boatman, had beaten A-tye, a tanka girl,
down at the harbour landing, and knocked an ear-ring, value a shilling,
out of her ear. They had previously reviled each other, and given
one another dreadful characters, in consequence of a collision. Lun
hit her with a bamboo, didn't mean it, and was very sorry. He was
to pay her a dollar—a decision which seemed to please them all.
Next, Wang, a hawker, was charged by a policeman with hawking
rice in the market without a license. But Wang kept a wood shop

and a shop is as good as a license, so the policeman was reprimanded, and Wang discharged. I then went with Mr. Mitchell over to the prison. Everything very clean and airy. The convicts were breaking granite for the roads, under a shed. Some, who had tried to escape, were ironed: some, who had tried twice, were doubly ironed. In one room I saw the terrible young American pirate, Eli Boggs, of whom Mr. Wingrove Cooke gives so interesting an account. He was a slim smart-built young fellow, about twenty-six—very good looking, with long dark hair, and a very remarkable eye, almost round, with a large pupil like a black bead. He complained terribly of his confinement, and said his chest was affected. I felt his pulse, and found it beating over 90. Here I also saw the Jack Ketch, a mild-looking man enough. Then went on in my chair to Mr. Davies' to lunch. His bungalow has the usual pretty view of the harbour and mainland, overlooking other bungalows, with very luxuriant gardens of bamboos and beautiful creepers. Mrs. Davies complained sadly of the want of milk, cream, and butter in Hong Kong, but was becoming reconciled to it. A nice little baby was suffering, as all the English children here do, from prickly heat. The road down into the town from this part lies entirely amongst bungalows and gardens—one part of it being very like the road at Vico, between Sorrento and Castel-a-mare, in the Bay of Naples. Heard, on my return, that one of our ships had gone off on "Pirate pigeon." Sat on the steps of the club watching the passersby. Close by the club is a clump of trees, which I have christened "Barber's Grove." The people are being shaved there, by many barbers, all day long. They also sell a fruit here, called the Chinese gooseberry. When cut through, its section is like a star; and it is not particularly nice. Also pears, quite round, and without any flavour; also a fruit, red in colour, with a thin skin, called a persimon, tasting something like an egg plum. In other baskets were plantains and pineapples; and a travelling *restaurateur* was selling a broth at "two cash a cup"—considerably less than a farthing. I was pleased by a visit from Mr. Chambers (in the house of Lyall, Still, and Co.), an old English friend. We walked with Mr. Anstey along the parade ground, and the latter told me an odd anecdote connected with the doubtful results of the missions here. A Chinaman had been hung at Hong Kong a short time ago, and the missionaries of different creeds had all fluttered down on him to claim the lost sheep as their own. The man had a notion, that by the English law, a condemned criminal may have whatever he wishes to eat and drink. He said to the missionary who appeared highest in favour, "My wanchey (*I want*) facey washey," meaning baptism. This was done, and then when asked to explain his reasons for this, he replied, "My wanchey roast duck." This not being complied with he died a Buddhist. The story requires no comment.

In the night rain fell with a violence I had never before witnessed. *Tuesday, 24th.*—The rain had not reduced the heat much, and the thermometer showed the temperature of the water in my jug and bason to be 84°. At 8 the washerman brought home my things, very fairly done, but a little knocked to pieces. Their mode of starching is not agreeable—they fill their mouths with rice water, and spirt it

over the fronts, collars, &c. M. Babtista, a Portuguese artist, called
and showed me some clever sketches, one of which—a view of Hong
Kong from the heights—I told him to finish for the Egyptian Hall.
At 1, on board the *Ganges*—the P. and O. boat starting with the mail
for England. It looked very pleasant to see the red Southampton
ticket, on the chairs and packages. A son of the late Mr. William
Murray, of the Edinburgh theatre, was returning by this mail. I had
a letter of introduction to him from Mr. Shortrede, of the *China Mail*
(since dead), and was sorry he was leaving. But he introduced me to
his brother, who remained at Hong Kong, and who proved a very
agreeable acquaintance.

To-day I took another long stroll about the town, by myself. They
are holding a Chinese *fête* in honour of their dead relations. They
keep firing crackers all day in the streets, and burning those long pastiles, the joss-sticks, we can buy in London. I don't think they care
much about their religion; they go into their temples to get cool, or
sit down, or go to sleep. The children are frightened at the gods,
they are so hideous; they roar with terror when they are placed in
front of them. The people walk about in the joss-houses with their
hats on, and whistle and smoke, and do what they like; the merchants
selling gilt paper and pastiles sit round the sides, and sometimes they
beat a gong to attract customers. They also keep burning paper imi-
tations of clothes, shoes, money, junks, etc., to help their dead friends
on their journey. I passed a little street of cook-shops. Here they
chop everything they sell into little bits, with onions and herbs, and
put them into a *cornet* made of a dried leaf—the same as used for
fans. The women were marketing, buying eggs, fruit, etc. One
bought half a duck, which was also cut up into little bits, head and
all. A *traiteur* was making a stew of fat pork and tripe, and at all
the shops were little heaps of fowls' entrails, and giblets, to sell. They
cut these things up upon blocks, with a sharp chopper, which they
hammered with their fists. *Everything* is sold by steelyard weight,
from fowls to onions.

Coming back to the club, I met Mr. Gilbert, of the *Surprize*. He
was in the action with the pirates, yesterday, off Lin-Tin. They
"pilled" twenty-five junks—burned eighteen, and brought seven
away to sell, with all their brass guns, etc. He cut the pigtail off one
of the pirates, and gave it to me.

At 7 to dine with Mr. Fischer, the Peninsular and Oriental Company's
agent at Hong Kong. His son-in-law, Mr. Scarth—an excellent artist
by the way—told me he once saw 150 people beheaded on the
execution ground at Canton, at the time of the rebellion. Their
hands were tied behind them, and a wooden ticket, explaining their
crime, was stuck down the back of their necks, and another on their
coiled-up pigtails. An assistant came up and took out the first
ticket, and lifted up their hands, which threw their heads forward :
then the executioner decapitated them at one *swish* with a sword. The
ground was plashy with blood, and when it was all over, a China
woman drove in a quantity of pigs to feed!

Wednesday, 25.—While at breakfast heard a monotonous chant
going on in the street, so went to the balcony. A Lascar funeral was
passing. Just as they got opposite the club one of the mourners.

suddenly punched another's head, upon which a general row began at once, and they broke one another's umbrellas into splinters. The remainder of the procession still went on singing their hymn, but looking back at the fight, until, at last, they all started once more together. Paid a visit to Messrs. Negretti and Zambra's photographer, M. Rossier, who lived at the Commercial Hotel, belonging, I believe, to Messrs. Lane and Crawford. He complained much of the effect of the climate on his chemicals. Up to the Police Court. Mr. Mitchell was hearing the case of a man who had stolen a woman's blouse and trowsers, hanging up to dry outside a house of by no means a doubtful character, in the Hollywood-road. The woman examined, who looked about 11, said she was 16, and was the servant of the house. She had been originally bought for fifteen dollars, and now had half a dollar a month. She added that she had never gone wrong. The prisoner said the things blew down, and he took them away. He had been before convicted, so he had three months hard labour, which also included a whipping— eighteen lashes when he went in, and eighteen when he came out. Mr. Mitchell told the girl, if they tried to lead her astray in the house, she was to come to him. She was, however, hideously ugly. Several cases followed, connected with Tai-ping-shang, the worst quarter of Hong Kong—perfectly unfit to record. Came home, and off in a boat to Mr. Jardine's, at East Point ; I was fortunate enough to find him at home. Then to Mr. Fischer's, where I had the pleasure of making the acquaintance of General von Straubenzee ; and then on board the *Calcutta,* to lunch with Lieutenant Walker. Come home to write, but people kept calling on me so, that I could not get through a line. At seven, to dine with Mr. Mitchell and Mr. Green, appointed Attorney-General during Mr. Chisholm Anstey's dismissal. Here I tasted shark's-fin soup for the first time. Home late ; all the sentinels about the streets, and the Chinese shut up in their houses, as usual, after eight. The crickets made such a noise in the trees I could hardly get to sleep.

A peculiar feature in the society of Hong Kong is, that everybody pitches into everybody else, and each says the other will be of no use to me. I should state that, from several gentlemen I met here, I derived most valuable information ; but from the majority it was difficult to get any practical hints respecting the native habits of the people themselves — those small prominent traits about which the public most care. The young men in the different large houses have a sad mind-mouldering time of it. Tea-tasting, considered as an occupation, does not call for any great employment of the intellect: and I never saw one of the young clerks with a book in his hand. They loaf about the balconies of their houses, or lie in long bamboo chairs ; smoke a great deal ; play billiards at the club, where the click of the ball never ceases, from earliest morning: and glance vacantly over their local papers. These journals are mostly filled with the most uninterestingly incomprehensible, and infinitessimally unimportant local squabbles, in which the names of Mr. Anstey, Mr. Bridges, Ma-chow-wang, Sir John Bowring, and Mr. Caldwell, are pitched about here and there, to the confusion of the stranger, who wonders at the importance attached to these storms in tea-cups, about which we never hear, or care, one-tenth part of a cash worth in England.

Thursday, 26th.—A dreary idiot wrote something in the *Friend of China*, to-day, about my visit to Hong Kong, and my "Book of Snobs"— Mr. Thackeray's, by the way—and Hong Kong Gents, and the 'Hong Hong style'—but all so cloudily local that I could not make head or tail of it—whether it was complimentary or abusive. Called on Sir John Bowring at Government House, finely situated on the hills. We had a pleasant chat about former literary friends, and were joined by Mr. Rutherford Alcock, our consul at Canton, and Captain McCleverty, of the *Cambrian*. Sir John gave me a little orange from Siam, not bigger than a bullet, but of excellent flavour. At two, Mr. Rozario, the police interpreter, called on me: and I arranged with him to be my companion, during my stay in China. He brought me two long matchlocks from Mr. Mitchell, taken in the junk-hunt last week. Started off with Rozario to shop, and bought many "properties" for the Egyptian Hall. We then went to a Chinese Restaurant. The lower room was the second class one, but the upper one was very nicely fitted up, with panels carved *au jour*, and painted and gilded recesses, for private parties and opium smokers. We sat down at a little table, and presently they brought us tea. There were already on the table five or six little saucers, some holding soy, and others little condiments and mixtures of mustard, spices, &c. The tea was put into the cups, and water poured on it. Then they covered the cup with the saucer, which fitted into it : and thus you strained the leaves back from the tea, when you drank. I thought our London tea much better—but everything in London is the best. We next had a little course, in saucers, of cakes, preserved pumpkin, some very little forcemeat puddings, and little paste bags of chopped pork fat. The wine was warm, and they poured it out of little pewter teapots, into small glasses that held about three thimblefulls. This repast—it was not a dinner—for Rozario and myself, with eight cash for the waiter (an hundred cash make fourpence) was only a shilling. There was a notice, in Chinese, up in the room, that the proprietors would not be responsible for anything stolen, and we copied this for the Hall.

In the afternoon, I got a boat, and went paying visits about the harbour—first to see Captain McCleverty, and a young cousin, a middy, on board the *Cambrian*, then to the *Calcutta*. Neither the Admiral nor the Captain were on board, but Mr. Cecil Mitchell was excessively polite, and I joined the ward-room mess. One of the officers showed me a snake-fish—a perfect serpent : another had a spider with a regular trap-door to his cell, and an insect from Australia, which burrows half way into the ground, and two sprouts, like grass, grow from it. The "prickly heat" worried me very much to-day, and my forehead felt like sand-paper. A violent rain to-night.

Friday, 27th.—A nice cool morning—thermometer down to 78°. To breakfast at Sir John Bowring's, walking up pretty winding paths, with the wild convolvulus and bamboo blooming all the way. Found him in the garden, with a native, gathering flowers for the table. He showed me a specimen of the "ribbon bamboo," close up by the house, every section of the cane bearing a different stripe : also the plant, from the pith of which they make what is wrongly called " rice paper." He told me there was one at Kew. Sallied out into the low parts of the town, with Rozario, in the afternoon : and bought a quantity of odd common crockery, " joss pigeon," stamped papers, &c. At seven to dine with Mr. Dixon, of the *China Mail*, meeting the Editor, Mr. Wilson, Dr. Chaldecott, and Mr. Douglas Lapraik, who told me that the Chinese junk, which visited us in 1848, was partly his specu-lation : but that he never received a halfpenny of the returns.

Saturday, 28th.—Early this morning my purchases began to arrive, including two of the large camphor wood chests they make and sell here, which are admirable to protect clothes, &c., kept in them from the moths. I set to work, with quantities of paper-shavings, and began to pack, during which Sir John Bowring called for a chat, and told me of some quaint places to visit when I got to Canton. Then to an opium sale with Mr. Lapraik and Mr. Crawford, the auctioneer. It was salvage 'opium—damaged by sea water. There were twenty balls, somewhat smaller than Dutch cheeses, in each box, and the first lots sold for two hundred and thirty-six dollarsa   box, which was accounted a good price. The buyers were nearly all fat Chinese *compradors*, or stewards, and they were very excited. The auctioneer talked pigeon-English to them. Then to Lindsey's, the bankers, for some money, where an independent clerk—a Hong Kong swell, I suppose—kept me waiting longer than ever I was kept anywhere before, without having the common civility to ask me to sit down. He wanted a mild course of Coutts's.

This afternoon I went to a great Chinese dinner, given by A-chung, the comprador to the Peninsular and Oriental Company at Hong Kong, a man reported to be worth £30,000 or £40,000. Captain Rogers, of the *Norna*, Captain Brooks, and Mr. Sutherland, met me at the office, and then we went on to A-chung's house, and up a ladder staircase, to the room where the comprador and two friends received us. They were jolly-looking fat old gentlemen, dressed in white. This is a plan of the room :—

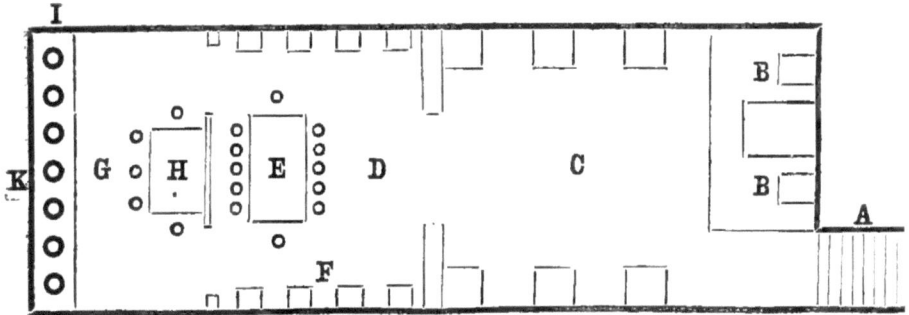

A. The ladder staircase of entry.
B. The couch for the opium smoking.
C. An ante-chamber.
D. The *salle à manger*.
E. The table, with stools round it.

F. Where the musicians sat.
G. A terrace in the open air, overlooking the sea.
H. A table with brandy, soda, pale ale, and cigars.
I. Flowers in pots on the edge of the terrace.
K. Hong-Kong harbour.

They received us with great courtesy and welcome. Our first ten minutes passed in looking about the rooms, at the furniture and appointments, lanterns, flower-baskets, &c. The dining-table was round, and laid out for a dozen, with a white cloth over it. Each guest had a large saucer; a smaller one with soy; another with a little glass or cup in it, and a porcelain spoon: also two chopsticks. Then we went out on to the terrace, which commanded the shipping in the harbour, and here we were introduced to the lady professional singers. These were three grown girls, with their hair wonderfully and elaborately dressed, and a smaller one, about eleven, with her head almost cropped, except a comical perpendicular fringe over the top, where our English girls wear a plait. They stared at us with their dull leaden faces, but made no attempt to return our salutation, and then all burst into a roar of laughter.

We now came back to the dining-room, where had arrived an orchestra of five performers—the men-servants of the compradors. The women played harsh stringed instruments, and the men the most screeching fiddles I ever imagined. They sang a song, with an accompaniment which Rozario told me was a sort of " *Mourir pour la patrie*" of the last revolution. It lasted many minutes: and appeared very like what I had heard at Singapore. The dinner then began. We had, in succession, sharks fins: a stew of goose: tendons of deer: birds nest soup: turtle: ham (very good): fowls and quails: pigeons made up like faggots: fish sounds: small puddings of pork fat, as at the eating house: a soup of rose leaves, with a strong twang of garlic: and many unknown things. There were *sixteen* courses. The women sat down with us, but did not eat anything: they had dined before, but they kept filling out little glasses with wine and samshoo perpetually. We ate as much as we could, for politeness, but soon knocked up. Then we broke up for another concert, and smoke, on the terrace; and then they asked Rozario "if that A No. 1 *sing-song-pigeon-man* (meaning me) could not do anything." So I showed them some few conjuring tricks, also the thimble-rig with three nutshells, and finally bewildered them all by singing the duet with the hand made up like an old woman, which I used to do in the scene of Baden fair. They could not make this out at all, and came behind the board that made the theatre to see if there was not a figure there. When I painted the hand of one of the girls to show her how it was done, they screamed with delight. In an hour another feast began, and they lighted all the lanterns. The meal was a prolonged desert of preserves and cakes, with fruit. The women sang at intervals, and Rozario accompanied them on the drum. Then we had speeches, with three times three. Then Mr. Sutherland proposed "the ladies," and on this being explained to "Tye-yow," our *prima donna*, she returned a few words in a really graceful and unaffected manner, observing that she and her friends felt complimented at being permitted to meet so many English mandarins. We broke up about half-past nine, with many compliments and good wishes on both sides. It was altogether a very novel and interesting affair. We got on pretty well with the chopsticks, but they had knives and forks and spoons in readiness, and when we left one of the compradors was getting pretty "tight" with pale ale.

Sunday, 29th.—Very seedy, with the fun of the night before, and did not get up until ten. Went out in the afternoon with Rozario. Half the shops were shut up—not from its being Sunday, as they recognise no Sabbath of any kind—but because the owners had been ordered back to Canton by the mandarins. The compradors, however, had all remained. I heard they are considered, by the Chinese, of such a low *caste*, they are hardly included in the census. They are, however, intelligent men of business. The tanka population, always living in their boats, on the water, are exempt from many of the laws applying to house-dwellers.

Went on board the *Calcutta* about two, and luckily caught Captain Hall on board, who introduced me to Sir Michael Seymour, who gave me an interesting map of Canton, and hoped we should meet there. He starts to-morrow morning. Then to dine in the ward-room; and had a long home talk with Lieutenant Mitchell about Chertsey, Englefield Green, and old friends, which was pleasant so far away. The officers gave me one or two fans, which a prince had presented them with, during their visit to Japan. Over the ship with Douglas Walker. They brought me back in the boat, and as I left the fellows began to bathe, and took splendid headers from the deck level, outside, and over three tiers of guns. We landed at a wharf, passing a family living in something like a large dog-kennel upon posts. The houses along here were all of blue brick, but with gay cornices and shutters, and frescoes under the eaves. Whilst writing, at night, a large specimen of the *blatta orientalis* flew through the window at my face with a force that really hurt me; and then went *whop* against the lamp and broke his head nearly off. Threw him out of window.

Monday, 30th.—To the Police-office, where Mr. May was conducting an inquest, and the body was lying in the street on a stretcher, for the people to look at. Then to call on the Lord Chief Justice, Judge Hulme, living out by East Point, in a large house that wanted a little repair. I experienced the usual courtesy, in my reception by this gentleman, who is very popular in the colony; but a recent domestic affliction had kept him for a while from visiting. Then, next door, to lunch with Captain and Mrs. Twiss. He took me to see a man very clever at bamboo-work, to whom I gave some orders. In the afternoon, went with Rozario to inspect a bankrupt joss-house, up by the Hollywood Road. Round the interior were many small figures, representing the tortures of the Buddhist hell. Some were being sawn in half between two boards: others burnt, or boiled in oil: others rung to death inside large bells. This was a purely Chinese quarter of the town, swarming with a native population, and bearing a terribly bad character.

At 7·30 to dine with Mr. John Dent, whose French cook sent up one of the best dinners I ever sat down to, in London or Paris. A claret cup was also a thing to recollect. Bets, and horses, and yachts formed the topic of conversation: and Hong Kong races were already on the *tapis*.

Tuesday, 31*st.*—Packing up all the morning for my first lot of baggage home : sawing off all the handles from the arms that had been given to me, and getting them bound together for transit. In the afternoon drew up my first "scheme" of my entertainment, and wrote part of my quick song. To-day Mr. Dent gave me several of Chinnery's sketches—very excellent authorities. Was called on to-day by several troublesome friends, who had evidently nothing to do, and came to hear what *I* had got to say, and not to tell *me* anything.

At four, Rozario came, and we started in chairs to the "Happy Valley," by a road cut through the neck of a ridge leading to a plain opening prettily on to the sea. This is the Hong Kong race course. There is a grand stand, and behind it, on the western side, are cemeteries, Catholic, Protestant, and Indian, or Parsee. The English church is temporary, of matting and bamboo ; the old one, behind it, having fallen in. An English cemetery, very far from home, has a very touching aspect. Many of the monuments were for those who had died here on board ship, from disease or in action. Many were mounted with obelisks, and capstans, and anchors, all carved in granite. Then on, up the valley, coming to a little Chinese school, supported by the English, with the pupils at small desks, and the old schoolmaster in the corner. It was a very pleasant sight. There were English maps and alphabets round the wall ; and the boys had little double paper books, with Indian ink tablets and pencils. One boy read his Chinese lesson to me, from his book, reading from top to bottom, in a sing-song voice. There was a pretty little village near here, buried in charming foliage, to which two small Chinese urchins were carrying water on a pole, followed by two smaller still, whose hats almost covered them. We walked on with fine *cacti* making hedges, and belts of mango and lychee trees. Here and there, water rushed down over blocks of granite, with a charming Chamouni sound about it. Kept right round the bend of the race-course, skirting a native cemetery, with quantities of bits of yellow paper blowing about, which are distributed at Chinese funerals to keep the ghosts quiet. Ferns grew plentifully about, and the foliage everywhere was delicious. As we turned to come back, we met several equestrians, and people in carriages, out for their afternoon ride. The whole place was so tranquil, and pretty, and home-like, that I got very low-spirited, and did not care to talk all the way back. A solitary English hearse going to the cemetery, with nobody to follow it, did not improve the spirits.

In the afternoon to dine with Sir John Bowring, meeting, besides the ladies of his family, Colonel Caine, Mr. Bridges, Mr. Bowring, jun., the Rev. Mr. Gray, of Canton, and others. In the evening came up the Bishop of Victoria, and his lady, with some other English residents. We had some music : and I was astonished to find how fresh some of my old songs came out. It was a very agreeable evening.

Wednesday, September 1.—Mr. Rutherford Alcock, our consul at Canton, sent a chair for me to go and breakfast with him—ham and eggs, shrimp curry, and very good tea. It appears odd to mention these little things, but well cooked dishes are not the rule here just at present. Up the hill with Mr. Morel, the Admiralty agent, to call on Captain and Mrs. Heaton. A very charming house and garden, with thick foliage over the walks, and a rill of water gurgling through the grounds, with an open bathing-place, surrounded by cane and matting. A very pretty little China maid, who spoke English, (not pigeon) very well, waited upon us at lunch. The air was filled with dragon flies, which they say presages a typhoon. To-day, Sir John Bowring sent me a curious scroll, and a packet of the convolvulus seeds ; and the Rev. Mr. Robinson brought me some quaint pith jars with paper bouquets. In the afternoon, strolling about the town I came upon one of our entertainers of Saturday, who kept an apothecary's shop. I sat down, and had some tea with him on a tub. The Chinese people were buying remedies, and I very much amused the two pigtail shopmen, showing them how we put up powders in England. They had pestles and mortars like ours, and they made pills as big as marbles. They did not bolt these when they took them, but bit pieces off.

To dinner with Mr. Kingsmill—a legal gentleman here, in good practice—with Mr. Mitchell, Mr. Chambers, Captain Twiss, and Mrs. Kingsmill. In the evening we had some very excellent music, and to a first-rate piano. They sang Pearsall's " Hardy Norseman " capitally ; and several glees, standing all round, in the approved style, with little books in their hands, when they ask—as I have seen men do at home—the shepherds why Cynthia did not love them, with a fa la la. A very charming evening, and I did not get back to the club till midnight.

Thursday, 2.—To breakfast with the Bishop of Victoria—an amiable and enlightened man. He was formerly the Rev. George Smith, attached to the China Mission, and wrote a good book on China, which he gave me, as well as the Litany printed in Chinese. Went over his college with him, which is attached to his palace. In the school-room was a small urchin, of six, in a pigtail, who did not like his book, and roared dismally. He had been removed from a girls' school, because he had been badly brought up, and used dreadful language before them. We had a talk about the Protestant mission, and I formed my own notions of its practical success. Then home, and to pack my second large box. Out in the harbour, at twelve, to call on an old Laleham friend, Mr. Barras, now commanding the *City of Carlisle*. Lunched with him and his wife, and two little girls, and looked over his books, among which I found a copy of Gay's *Fables*, given to him by Mrs. Fox (widow of Charles James Fox), who used to be very kind and play the harp to me when I was a little boy, at St. Anne's Hill. It is strange how these small *souvenirs* of early home affect you, when so very far away. To us arrived three visitors—captains of Opium clippers,—with one of whom I went over the *Bombay Castle*. Then on board the *Adventure*, to dine with Lieutenant Gilbert. Was cheered by the old friends of the *Norna* as we passed her, which led to an exchange of chaff with Soy and Fleetwood. We sat down to an excellent dinner on board the *Adventure*, with nothing to complain of but the close atmosphere. We had coffee on deck, from which the view of Hong Kong, with the lights rising up the hill, was charming—looking more like Portici and Resina from the Bay of Naples, than ever. The sea was very phosphorescent, but not more so than I have seen in Boulogne Harbour.

To-night was very sultry, and, although tired as usual, I could not sleep for the heat, and rolled all my musquito curtains up, in despair.

Friday, 3rd.—To breakfast with Mr. Anstey, who told me the whole of the "Robinet affair" which is creating a great excitement here—and told it very well. Robinet was a merchant here—he insured a great quantity of silk bales, in a ship, for Lima, and started with them. The ship caught fire, mysteriously, on the way: and when they opened some of the bales by accident, they found there was no silk in them, but only 'gunny-bags,' made of matting. Then Robinet was so affected, he told the captain two or three times he should commit suicide; but the captain hoped he would not, so he gave it up. At last, just before they reached Lima, they found the cabin empty, with a note left, saying that he had thrown himself overboard. But, unluckily, somebody met him, a day or two afterwards, in the streets at Lima; and he had been brought back to Hong Kong to await his trial. I heard that many people made good 'pigeon' here, by getting a cargo on credit, and then borrowing money on it!

To lunch with Captain Hall, in the *Calcutta*, who gave me a curious native map of the ninety-six pirate islands; and then said he would give me some Chinese costumes, if I would lecture for the benefit of the Cancer Hospital, at Brompton, when I got back. It was a bargain. He told me a good plucky story about his early connection with this institution, from the circumstance of a cancer having arisen from an abrasion of his lip, from playing the cornet-à-piston; and some very interesting circumstances connected with its removal and cure.

In the evening, Mr. Sutherland borrowed Mr. Scarth's little Croydon basket-carriage, and we drove along the 'Happy Valley,' and past Mr. Jardine's, at East Point, along the Limoon Passage—the northern entrance to Hong Kong harbour. Granite rocks coming nearly down to the sea—water rills falling—Chinese graves, and fishing stations, all the way. Many people out in carriages, and some Yankees in light iron four-wheeled trotting gigs; also a string of Mr. Jardine's horses, led out for airing by black grooms. At dinner, at Mr. Seare's, I met Mr. Cleverly, who escaped, with his thigh shot through, and the bone badly comminuted, from the massacre on board the *Queen* steamer, and swam for an incredible time, until picked up by a lorcha. It is terribly hot to-night. I am finishing up my diary, in my room, in the costume of an ancient statue—the crickets wearing themselves out with creaking, and the click of billiard balls, and perpetual cries of "Boy!" sounding all over the club.

Saturday, 4th.—A smoking morning, and the hills in a steam of heat. Too beaten to go out, so kept on packing. Captain Hall sent the dresses; Mr. Babtista brought me the water-colour drawings for my scenery; and Rozario came with a barber's stool he had purchased in the street. Went out with him about four, and up to the joss-house on the Hollywood Road. It was a festival. They had put some most hideous josses, large and small, outside the temple, dressed in tawdry gilt paper clothes. Inside, these clothes were displayed on bamboo frames like tailor's dummies, for the people to buy and burn for their dead relations. There were also for sale, fruits, cakes, and joss candles. Sailors and strangers were walking in and out and pulling about the "altar-pigeon" as they pleased; and children were knocking the bells with canes, for fun. There were lanterns placed on poles outside to mark the limits of the joss's division; and the ghosts who wandered outside these limits did not derive any benefit from the things burned. I perceived none of the people believed in, or cared one straw for, all these ceremonies. Rozario took me over several of the lowest of the low lodging houses in this quarter of Hong Kong, and in one of them I saw a woman with little feet, who after much fuss, removed the shoe. We gave her a dollar, but she did not appear to know what to do with it. To dine with Mr. and Mrs. Bridges, meeting Mr., Mrs., and Miss Day, and Mr. and Mrs. Lyall. We had a frog curry, which was excellent. Mr. Bridges mentioned that Mr. Legge, a missionary, had told him, with regard to the antiquity of China, that people in remote villages had showed him incontrovertible pedigrees going back to *before the Flood*. And Mr. Lyall told me that at an execution he saw at Hong Kong, a vast number of women wailed under the scaffold with terrible energy, all dressed in deep mourning (white): but that the minute the drop fell, they threw all their mourning off, bundled it up under their arms and went away laughing. They were all hired.

Sunday, 5th.—Not very well all day from the great heat, and was obliged to lie down on my bed. Much better when the sun fell. To dine with Mr. John Dent, meeting Colonel Foley, Military Secretary at Canton, and Mr. William Dent, who, in his beard, is constantly taken for me. (*Mem:* Last night we had port-wine and cayenne, with roast goose—a good thing: to-night we had fine prawns as a nice garnish to boiled fish). I heard in conversation, the Chinese never allow themselves to be beaten. They pretend to know already all you tell them, usually replying, "Can savey that pigeon, Pekin sye."

At 8 p.m., the mail gun banged in the harbour, and in one hour afterwards the "Home News" came up. Nothing particularly interesting to me, except an account of the laying of the first stone of the New Adelphi Theatre.

Monday, 6th.—At six this morning my boy, A-Pow, came in with all my papers and letters from home. All good news, and felt very jolly. Babtista came to be paid this afternoon, and made me a present of a large toy, representing a sing-song, which I took to pieces very carefully and packed up. Dined with Mr. Sherman, at the hospital. Very pleasant, and a great deal of talk about London and mutual friends.

Tuesday, 7th.—A great wind in the night, which blew my blinds about terribly. Took a long walk, finishing at my bamboo man's, at Spring-gardens, who is making my proscenium, for the Hall, very prettily. Home with some coolies, who took my boxes over to the P. and O. office, and Mr. Sutherland kindly saw them all properly "fixed." With Rozario, to get some queer things—locks and lanterns and umbrellas, at a shop just opened in Tai-ping-shang. To dine with Sir John Bowring, meeting Sir Charles and Lady van Straubenzee, Captain and Mrs. van Straubenzee, Mr. Jardine, Sir Michael Seymour, Captain Hall, and others. We were joined in the evening by Colonel

c 2

Kennedy, Colonel Caine, Mr. Forth, Captain Brooker, Mr. Days, Mr. Bridges, &c. Good conversation never ceased, and we had great fun about some wine that Sir John had received from Japan, than which nothing could be nastier. There is a report, to-night, from Sir Robert Maclure, that the Chinese are shuffling about the treaty. At night, coming home, all the chairs and their lanterns, following one another down the winding-path to the town, had a pretty effect.

Wednesday, 8th.—Off to Canton. Packed up and started at noon, in the *Fei-maa* (*Flying Horse*) steamer, for Macao. Amongst many hills and islands, green and pleasant. The Captain—Castella—"A No. 1, piecey-man." At dinner, about three, guards were placed at the cabin-doors, and on deck, with swords, and loaded guns and revolvers; we also kept our own on the seats and tables near us ; for there were seventy Chinese on board, and much treasure. Passed the scene of the massacre on board the *Queen;* and also of the loss of the *Raleigh.* We arrived off Macao about four; and the row and noise and struggling of the tanka boat girls to get alongside was inconceivable—even to fighting with oars and boat-hooks, and cutting adrift each other's boats that made fast to the sponsons, with choppers. Up to Mr. William Dent's, on the Praya. Amused ourselves with shooting clay pellets from the verandah, at the dogs; and then round the sea-road for a stroll, to the back of the island, passing some cemeteries, and the cave of Camoens. Macao has very little of China about it. It is shaped like Weymouth, but with its cathedrals and buildings might be like any foreign Catholic town. Lots of clear cool drinks at dinner, and to bed, tired.

Thursday, 9th.—Up at five, and with our party to bathe in a pretty little bay, with a good sand and pebbly bottom. We each went in a tanka boat; and our pretty boat-girls, who rowed us out, were not in the least degree put out by our ablutions and evolutions. My *batelière* was called A-Tye, and she had beautifully small hands and feet. The *Fei-maa* started again at 8.30, and at breakfast all the armed precautions were gone through as before; the guns and pistols being discharged afterwards, to show that they were loaded. We assed the Bogue Forts about noon, all knocked to pieces now, with the *Sanspareil* lying near the middle island. Then past Whampoa, where many ships were anchored. Here I first saw a pagoda, and then several others—some of them excessively picturesque, with foliage up to the very top. The boats thickened about the river as we approached Canton, which now, as seen from the river, is nothing more than a heap of ruins. When we stopped, at Honan, Mr. Fisher came on board to ask me up to Mr. Jardine's *Hong,* but I was bound for the Head Quarters. And now I saw pagodas, and josses, and Mandarin standards, and flower boats, and felt I was actually in the real China. Went off in a boat, down the river, with Captain Castella and Rozario to the Commissariat Gate, where we landed amidst crowds of English soldiers, principally belonging to the Bengal Infantry. At the south east gate we found Captain Duffin, Captain Montmorency, and some other officers quartered in a pagoda ; and they asked us to share their dinner—a very good one : roast pig, roast goose, beef, and champagne. I then went with Rozario along the eastern walls of the city to head-quarters. The walls are something like those of Chester, in their height above the city, with a walk on the top behind the embrasures. We passed, on our left, acres and acres of brickbats—also the remains of the Examination Hall, which consisted of rows of little rooms, like cattle-sheds, running closely parallel, to the amount of some hundreds, into which the candidates were shut for their examinations. Passed other pagodas inhabited by French and English troops, for another mile and a-half, and then to head-quarters, pleasantly situated on the slope of a finely wooded hill. Here I found General Van Straubenzee, in a superb joss-house lately built and endowed by Yeh.* He received me most kindly, and as I could not find Major Travers (who had invited me to his quarters), insisted on my stopping where I was, putting up a light bed for me on the top balcony, with joss-rooms adjoining, and commanding a fine prospect. Went for a little walk with him, to another joss-house—in fact, the Head Quarters appear to be a perfect *monte sacro*—from the balcony of which we obtained a splendid view of the city, chequered with trees and pagodas, and especially ruins, everywhere. It reminded me very much, with the river and the trees in the distance, of the view from the Fourvières, at Lyons. Back to a bath, and then to dinner in the temple—the party consisting of Captain Van Straubenzee, Major Travers, Mr. Harry Parkes, the commissioner, Captain Fisher of the Engineers, and myself. Colonel Foley was so good as to help me rig up my mosquito curtain, when I went to bed about eleven. I could not sleep for some time, from the mere actual excitement of feeling that I was at last *inside Canton!* The evening was intensely hot, my thermometer standing at 91°, and the air perfectly still. The vast silent city below, glooming through the starlight, was most impressive.

Friday, 10*th.*—Up at six, and wandered about the joss-house, and then wrote. After breakfast went up the hill and through another temple to a grass perch on the mound above the walls, whence there was a very pretty view of the country outside Canton on the north. To the right were the White Cloud Mountains; and below an expanse of cultivated land, with many villages, and clumps of trees, hills, cemeteries, broken ground, and rice fields, amongst which numerous peasants were bobbing for frogs. Along a great many paths people were coming from the country into Canton, and the scene altogether was very sunny and rural. On going back to the temple, I met the Bishop of Victoria, who had come up to a confirmation of the troops, and kindly called on me. There was a magnificent bell outside my room, and he translated the characters on it, to the effect that, with many flourishes, it had been given by Yeh in honour of the Joss.† At noon for a walk with Rozario, who knows Canton well, and was present at its capture; first round the walls, and then to the Five-storied Pagoda, where the Mossoo marines have established themselves. In front were two enormous red sandstone lions—Egyptian in size. Then by some Chinese shops with signs, "Best wash from Hong Kong," "Wash soap here," "Cheap Johndy," &c.

---

* Yeh is universally pronounced *Yep* in China. His name is *Yep-choon-ming.*
† This bell is now in the Crystal Palace at Sydenham, presented by General Van Straubenzee. It was brought over by Captain Maguire, in the *Sanspareil.*

To another beautiful joss-house—the quarters of the Engineers. The ascent to it was very fine—up heavy granite steps, with large trees on either side, rising with the staircase, which must have been very, very old. The gate had a most elaborate coating of animals, josses, aud trees, all in porcelain. Here resided Captain Fisher, who showed me some very remarkable subaqueous infernal machines, which the Chinese had made for the Canton river, and which blew up, at a given time, by clockwork. Saw a smashing fight between two turkeys, one of which we ate a few days afterwards. Captain Fisher told me he had a goose that could thrash both the turkeys sometimes, when he got loose. A very sharp and intelligent little China boy brought a shoulder of mutton and some ducks to Head Quarters, and I had a talk with him. He says he is coming to England, to learn "all sort pigeon." Rain and thunder in the afternoon: after which I went out on a clever piebald pony, with Captain Fisher, and Rozario. We called for some more fellows at the Engineer's Quarters, and then on, through narrow streets, to the *Yamun* (palace) of the Allied Commissioners, formerly the residence of the Tartar General. It was a wonderful place, with large court yards of steps and inclined planes, evidently made for horse processions ; and a court of justice, fitted up with beams and carvings of great beauty. Here we met Mr. Harry Parkes,* who collected four police, and some more friends, and then off on an expedition, all armed to the teeth. We may have been 14 or 15 in all. And now *through Canton.* The western city and suburb was first taken. The streets average about six feet in width, and were choked with people and their wares : all of whom were, more or less, burning joss-sticks before their shops to propitiate fortune. The trades appeared to get together in different streets. As Mr. Parkes observed, with us it is all opposition—with them, all combination. Large spiders sent their webs to join the opposite eaves over our heads, and then hung in the middle, like small bats ; and the gaudy sign boards hung all about, high and low. Few of the houses had more than one story. The shopmen and most of the people were naked to the waist. The quarters of the town were all divided one from another, the barriers being made by the heavy barricade poles that close some of the shops. The streets were paved with oblong slabs of granite, about three feet long by one broad. Very few women were about, except hideous old ones of the genus *Gamp :* and with their little feet they looked doubly repulsive. We went to the Temple of Longevity, riding our ponies up the steps and into the court-yard, getting there just as evening service was going on. They accompanied their mass on two instruments—a large gong, and a small sing-song drum. They stood before little mats laid on the ground ; and when they had done their chant the priests prostrated themselves before the grim idol several times. They were the most villanous-looking set of hope-abandoned thieves I ever saw. Their heads were shaved all over, consequently they wore no pigtails. Then into other parts of the temple, where were different josses, carved out of wood and gilt, each one more awfully ugly than the last. From a gallery at the top of the temple,

---

* Now Consul at Shanghae.

called "The Retreat of the Dragon," we had a famous view of the head quarters. Lastly, into the gardens of the joss, which, with its pavilions and trees and bridges, struck everybody as ".very like the old willow-pattern plate."

We now went on through many more streets, each so exactly like the last, that it was difficult to remember one from the other, to the "Temple of the Five Hundred Gods." And there *were* five hundred : all in rows, like the sculpture at the Royal Academy. They were about three or four feet in height, and bore every possible expression of face that could be conceived. (I was very much worried about this place, from a mysterious impression that I had seen it all before, years ago, and in a dream: even to knowing that if I went out at a certain door, there would be a garden. *And there was!* I do not in any way pretend to account for this, and I said nothing about it. I am not aware that I have ever seen any print, or representation, or description of it ; but that I recognised it as familiar, I am fixedly convinced. I leave psychologists to explain it). In the garden we saw many tubs of gold fish, of different shape to ours, with excessively remarkable tails and fins. They were tame, and would allow you to take them for a few seconds out of the water. There were also a large number of dwarfed trees—some trained into deer, and houses, and dolphins, with egg shells for eyes, as at Mr. Whampoa's, at Singapore. Some were very old ; amongst these were a bamboo, as thick as my wrist, trained backwards and forwards, like the serpent in an Egyptian *cartouche*, with young shoots. The lotus also grew in perfection, in huge pots and stagnant tanks. They sell its roots in the street, in bits like magnified ginger, or a cactus made of horse-radish. Its seed vessel lies on the top of the water, very like the rose of a large watering pot. Each of the Five hundred Gods appeared to have a special set of admirers, as we saw by the ashes of the joss-sticks before them, some of which were still burning. Still on, through streets and streets, and streets again, to a Guard House, wherein were shields with dreadful faces painted on them, and a representation of a rebel battle outside Canton. Everywhere we were offered tea. On again, over bridges and small canals, to the Execution Ground, a place very like the yards of warehouses, seen on leaving town by the Greenwich Railway. It was a potter's bit of waste ground ; but at executions the things were cleared away. Mr. Parkes told me that Mr. Scarth's anecdote about the pigs was quite true. He added that the friends of the superior criminals paid to take the heads and bodies away, but that the heads of the lower classes were all thrown together into a crate.

It was now getting dark : so we rode quickly up the street of Benevolence and Love, under triumphal arches, and between rows of ruins, to the parade ground, which we all crossed at full gallop—parted at the bottom of the hill, and then home after a wonderful day of surprise and interest.

Saturday, 11th.—The *reveillée* of fifes and drums, in the early dark morning when the city is so still, is very effective. This is soon answered by the French bugles from the Five-storied Pagoda. General Van Straubenzee left for Hong Kong at 7.30, so Colonel Foley and I breakfasted together ; and afterwards looked out and aired some fine flags, taken from the Tartar General's *yamun*. Out with Rozario and down to the river, where we embarked and paid Mr. Still a visit in his "chop," or floating office, off Honan. He was so good as to promise me the very dress that Yeh wore at the time of his capture. Then to lunch with Mr. Fisher and Mr. Whittall, in Messrs. Jardine's house at Honan, meeting the Rev. Mr. Gray. We then all started for the great Temple of Honan, through narrow streets, like those of Canton, with quantities of live fish exposed for sale, in pans of water. The temple covers an enormous extent of ground—acres on acres—and is approached by a large solemn court, shaded by huge trees. The priests, who knew Mr. Gray well, and respect him very much, were just going to dinner in a large refectory. The eldest chanted a grace, and a younger one accompanied him by knocking a bell, first offering a little rice to Buddha, with his chopsticks. We were then introduced to a bishop who was consecrated last week. There were a great many other temples and outbuildings on the ground—some for visitors, and travellers, with small sleeping cells. In several of these, they brought us tea : and in one, we opened a basket we had brought with us, and had some sherry, and brandy and water, giving the priests some ; but they did not appear to like it. Then I sang the Bishop a song, and we got capital friends. We then went into the gardens, which were like those of the Canton joss-houses, but much finer. In a large kitchen garden was a *columbarium*, as at Pompeii, containing the calcined bones of former priests, whose bodies had been burned, further on, at the place of cremation. Back to a plantation, where there was the largest tortoise I ever saw—three feet long, I dare say—and reported to be a thousand years old. One of the painted josses in the temple was uncommonly like Lord Brougham. As we returned through the streets to the wharf, the children shouted "*Fan-kwei*" (foreign devil) after us. It was now dark ; so I borrowed a lantern at the S.E. pagoda, and so home, challenged by the sentinels every twenty yards, " Who goes there ?" "A friend." "Advance, friend, and give the word." "France and England." "Pass, friend, and all's well."

Sunday, 12th.—To breakfast with Mr. Hannan, at the Artillery Barracks, close by. They had a little Chinese servant here, they called " Joss." He had been *found*, during the war, in a ruined house, with nobody belonging to him ; and afterwards a horse kicked his head open, and the doctor took out a quantity of his brains, which, oddly enough, from being excessively stupid, turned him into a sharp little boy. He waited very well and quietly ; and, as they all do, was constantly watching the table. I was very seedy with the heat this morning, and went to sleep in my balcony, until Rozario came, when I awoke. I went round to lunch with the engineers ; and then Captain Fisher, and the rest of us, armed, and started for "another go into Canton," on foot. One of the young officers knocked up from the heat soon after we set off, and fell into the rear. We went first to the Temple of the Great Bell, which was broken through, in the war, with a cannon-ball. In the garden was shown the print of Buddha's foot—an irregular pit hewn or worn in the sandstone, at the bottom of a tank. The impression was filled with stagnant water, and might have been eight or nine feet long. Then to the Temple of Horrors, where were representations of the tortures of the Buddhist hell—of similar meaning to, but better carried out than those in the joss-house at Hong Kong. The figures of the sufferers, executioners, &c., were barely three feet high, with singularly hideous but expressive faces. The features of those whose punishment was coming next, were very ludicrous. On the rocks at the side, were many smaller figures, but they were all in dark niches, and could not be seen very well. Then to the Temple of the Five Genii. In front of the altar here are placed the five petrified rams, who had something to do with the foundation of Canton, but I don't know what, nor is it important to remember. They were five irregular blocks of stone, perched on wooden legs. They might just as well have been called the five petrified potatoes, for any resemblance they had to anything. Canton is sometimes called the City of the Rams. We next crossed the river to Honan, and landing at the temple before visited, saw the sacred pigs, thirteen or fourteen in number, enormous in size, and blind with age. Then to take tea again with the priests. An old man, in huge spectacles, was rivetting some broken china, and chipping out the names of the owners on the inside of some basins. He had a row with the priests because he had put on the best, or copper rivets, instead of common metal ones ; upon which he took them all out, would not put in any more, and went away in a rage. Crossed the river again, and by the commissariat landing, through the city, buying scrolls, carved stones, kites, &c., for the Hall.

I saw several curious things to-day, in the streets and shops. They card their wool with a bow, like a huge fiddle-stick, which they knock with a mallet on the string, and the recoil catches up the wool. In a mill, they jumped upon the end of a lever, which let a heavy hammer fall on the grain, put into a stone bowl on an incline. They all work very hard. They weigh everything, as at Hong-kong—fish, wood, ducks, fruits, and so sell it. When they expose dead fish for sale, they rub fresh blood over it, to make it look fresh. The fish, however, are mostly sold alive, gasping on their sides, in shallow pans of water. I saw some very large and fine eels. Their weights are all steelyards. They dont like bating their price, and get very angry if asked, but they give you a *cum-shaw*, or present. The blocks of granite, which pave the streets, have a singularly smooth and polished appearance, from the naked feet and soft shoes so constantly shuffling over them.

Back to Head Quarters at 6.30, rather tired with a long day. To dine with Colonel Stevenson, who lives up at the top of the hill, with a clever bamboo balcony built out from his room. Captain Schomberg and Colonel Foley joined us. Had a long talk after diner about the Scots Fusiliers and old times in town. Home, with the Hindoo orderly carrying a lantern before us, and challenged as before by the sentinels.

Monday, 13th.—In a small procession, with Mr. Parkes, and the French commissioner, *marins*, soldiers, police, &c., to visit Pei-Kwei, the governor of Canton. Guns were fired as we entered the *Yamun*, and we rode up the stairs and through the different courts and gates. The old gentleman wore a long loose white silk (what looked like a) bedgown. He and Mr. Parkes bowed so long to one another before they went in at the door, that I thought we were never to enter. Then we all sat round a little table, and tea was brought in two-

handled pewter saucers. Then, as they were going to talk "pigeon"—
but Chinese pigeon—he sent me with a servant to see his house and
grounds. Everything in the palace was terribly out of repair—
and the grounds overgrown, the pavements splintered, the pavilions
rotting, and the private josses and altars overturned and broken. At
noon up to the Engineers, to lunch, and then out for another prowl.
Went to the Treasury first—a miserably dilapidated old place—
certainly beating everything in the way of neglect, short of actual
ruin, that ever I saw. We went carefully up a rotten staircase, to see
a hall wherein they found *thousands* of bats clinging to the rafters,
with guano a foot deep on the floor. But although the place was so
tumble-down, thousands of dollars were looted from the treasury.
In the grounds were large pieces of ornamental water, now dried up,
with ruined rockwork, and gardens choked with weeds and off-shoots.
There was a large park, almost impassable for the underwood, but
full of fine deer, which scampered away in all directions. All this was
in the middle of the city. Then again about the town, and amongst
the shops, the merchants always bringing us tea. Dined with the
Engineers, sitting next to Dr. Hawkins. Awfully hot at night, 89
degrees in my room.
  Tuesday, 14th.—Almost knocked up to-day, so decided upon going
over to Honan for a little change. This was the only day I really
felt poorly, and when I went down to the river, and across to Honan,
I could not sit up, but dozed off on the journey. I expect I have been
working in the sun a little too hard. To Mr. Jardine's go-down,
where Mr. Whittall and Mr. Fisher received me, and I had breakfast
with the Bishop of Victoria and Mr. Gray. After breakfast I lay
down on one of the beds and slept well until two, which pulled me up
capitally. The *Fei-maa* and *Willamette* steamers arrived from Hong
Kong, bringing, amongst others, Mr. Macleod (of Jardine's), who joined
us. About five, Mr. Whittall, Mr. Bryant, and myself, went up the
river in a boat, to see Puntinqua's gardens ; but it got dark too
soon. We landed at a little creek, where there was a water village,
all on piles, with many tanka-boats. We went up towards the gardens,
on irregular embanked paths between fields of rice, and walked along
the walls, but could not get in ; so I recommended a return, as it was
a nasty neighbourhood, and we were unarmed. To bed early, but
could not sleep from the heat, so wandered about the balcony. Below
us, was a little neighbourhood of family boats, and a child who cried
all night. At day-break they all burnt joss-paper for a propitious
day.
  Wednesday, 15th.—Better to-day. Mr. Gray, Mr. Phillips, Rozario,
and myself, started this morning, to Puntinqua's garden. On the
river a squall came on, and we were all very nearly blown over ; this
would have been awkward, as I was the only swimmer of the party.
Went up the creek of last night, and then changed into a *san-pan*
(a very slight boat), rowed by two little boys at about a mile an hour.
Up another slimy creek to Puntinqua's gate, and over the gardens.
The same story—all rotten and neglected, and tumbling to pieces.
I really believe that the reason for the Chinese having kept Canton so
jealously shut up for centuries was, that they were ashamed of it.
Here were huge dry lotus tanks, and bridges over ground, and

carved summer houses, and hard chairs, stone seats, and thin oyster-shell windows. The French had "looted" terribly here, and the old gardener complained bitterly of their excesses. They had broken the woodwork, and bent the copper enamel jars, and stolen and destroyed the pictures. In the women's rooms, however, were left some which might have had a curtain drawn before them with advantage. There was a well-built stage, for sing-song pigeon, and a pavilion for the women opposite to it, between which and the theatre water ought to have been. Determined to fit up the Hall somewhat in this style. In the gardens were many more of the dwarfed and trained trees, and apparently acres of lotus tanks and ponds. Then up the pagoda, amidst a quantity of rock work wired together, and over small bridges, and by cages for birds and serpents, all decaying, with the roofs falling in. The place altogether might have belonged to Tennyson's Moated Grange, and Hood's Haunted House. Some enormous pebbles, on wooden tripods, made cool, but uncomfortable seats. We now went back, down the stream, to Howqua's garden, which is on the Honan side of the river, on the way to Fatshan Creek. The boat-life here was extraordinary, and the majority appeared to be returning to Canton. We passed up a foul creek, by many nursery gardens, to Howqua's. The place was not so bad in its dilapidation as Puntinqua's—a little care would have put it decently to rights. The lotus-tanks were larger and clearer, and the rooms and kiosks in better repair; but still much was tumbling town. But both would be charming places, kept in the style of Dropmore.

Home about four, and my "prickly heat" was more fully out to-day than I had yet seen it. It is intolerable, but they say "so healthy." Up to dine with Captain Duffin, at the Pagoda, meeting Captain Castella there, and his brother-in-law, Mr. Cooper, who built the docks at Whampoa, and whose father was carried off and murdered by the Chinese, the year before last. They came alongside his *chop*, and said they had a letter for him; he stooped to take it, when they pulled him into the boat, and took him off, right under the guns of the English ships. We had a very capital dinner, and lots of really good fun. When we came down to the Allied Landing-place, at night, we found six pirates, that one of our boats had just taken, all squatting on the ground, tightly tied together by their pig-tails.

Thursday, 16th.—Started in the *Fei-maa* to Whampoa, to see Captain Heath. A storm of rain brought the temperature down several degrees, and the change was most delicious; but, as usual, the heat soon came back again, with increased intensity. When I got to Whampoa, Captain Heath had gone to breakfast with the French Admiral on board the *Audacieuse*, so I went on to Mr. Cooper's *chop*—a very large one—and had breakfast there. His mother and sister joined us. The old lady was very weary of China, and longed to be home again; and so did everybody else I met, except Mr. Gray, who loves China with all the affection of a *vaterland*. Back to the *Assistance*, to which Captain Heath had now returned. He was very glad to see me, and loaded me with presents, for the Hall. We then went to call on Captain Edgell, on board the *Tribune*, and afterwards paid a visit to the French Admiral, who had asked me to dinner, on board his ship, in Mr. Cooper's dock—an admirable and successful undertaking. Whilst we were going over the works a tremendous storm of rain came on, during which, as before, the breathing temperature was delicious, but steamingly hot afterwards. Back again to the *Assistance*, where we had luncheon, and yarned for a couple of hours about club affairs in London. Captain Heath has engaged a tanka-boat to himself, during his stay at Whampoa. She lays astern of the *Assistance :* and is peopled by one family—father, mother, little sister, and a boy. The little girl—about six or seven—had gone off to market, in a *san-pan ;* and was now returning with some pig and duck, chopped together in little bits ; also a fish. The woman was ill the other day, and the Whampoa doctor came to see her. They all wrangled a long time about his fee, which eventually, with physic and conjuring, came to sixpence. If the woman did not get better, he was to give it back again ; which I saw him doing. They had propitiated the joss to-day—a hideous little doll—with three small cups of tea, a hard pear, and a mouldy plantain. Their wages, altogether, were two-and-a-half dollars a-week.

Started for Canton, at half-past four, with Captain Edgell, on board the *Clown* gun-boat—(*Mem.* Good position for the Engineer's Story)—and home to Honan by six. Restless night, and a little feverish : drank a great deal of water.

Friday, 17*th.*—Dull close morning, and rather languid and pulled : could not eat anything, but drank all that came near me—tea, beer, water, &c. At half-past one with Mr. Macleod to lunch with Captain Edgell, in the *Bittern,* meeting Captain Colville, of the *Camilla,* and Lord Gilford. We were all going up to Head Quarters : but just as we started from the Commissariat Landing, the rain came on with such violence that the journey was given up. I then took a chair, and with Captain Colville walking, we came all through the western suburbs of Canton to the landing-place at Cha-ming, passing the sites of Hog Lane and Physic, or Old China, Street, at the back of which the old factories stood. Then on board the *Camilla,* where Captain Colville gave me a double-sword ; and back to Honan. My friends were getting ready to go to a dinner on board a flower-boat, on the river, close round the corner of the Fa-tee creek. The dinner was in the same style as that at A-chung's, at Hong-kong : and with similar dishes ; and the lady singers all wonderfully like one another ; with wooden and perfectly inexpressive features. There were five or six Chinese ; and the rest were English. I was more than ever impressed with what I have before put down—the almost remarkable ignorance of every feature and phase of Chinese life, peculiar to the "Commercials" out here. The Almighty Dollar, in its relations to tea, silk, and opium, is the only study, or source of thought, with them : and what they can possibly do, when left to themselves, to get through the day, beyond smoking and tea-tasting, is to me a matter of the most marvellous incomprehensibility.

The scene on board the Flower Boat, removing its English components, was novel and striking. The boats are those imitated in the Chinese bird-cages, and bear a questionable character. They are beautifully fitted up, with carving, glass, flowers, and lanterns, and have a striking appearance gliding about the river at night. The principal room is the *salle-à-manger,* and all have kitchens attached to them. There was an orchestra of instruments similar to those at Hongkong, and the songs appeared identical also. It was pleasant to sit on the open forecastle platform, and look at the brightly-illuminated tableau within; and the moon, the water, the numerous boats, with their lanterns, with the Canton pagodas in dark outline, made a very effective scene. Mr. Phillips joined us, and kindly explained one or two points to me, He is an able writer, and has studied the Chinese well. We broke up about half-past 12 ; rare dissipation for Canton.

Saturday, 18*th*.—Still all to pieces, and indisposed to do anything. Went to sleep on the floor, after breakfast, and slept till noon, when I got a boat, and crossed the river by myself, and so up to the Head Quarters. A long agreeable chat with Colonel Foley, whose rooms are masterpieces of taste and arrangement under difficulties. Then to General Van Straubenzee, who gave me a couple of glasses of port, which almost directly began to pull me up again. Packed up all my things, and got another chair to carry them. Rarely, I expect, had such a collection of "loot" and festive properties left Canton. First, to Mr. Still's *Chop*, when he gave me Yeh's coat—very handsome, and lined with a fine white silky fleece,—then strolled a little about Honan, and the children cried " *Fan-kwei*" again, after me— even the smallest shrimps and mudlarks of two years old. To bed early—very tired, but all right again.

Sunday, 19*th*.—On board the *Willamette*, a Yankee built steamer, for Macao and Canton, at nine. She has a hurricane deck and paddles, and the man steers from a little house on the forecastle. They gave us a capital breakfast, with some "A No. 1" American ham—most excellent, but spoiled in the cutting ; all people who spoil hams by making a gash at once into them, as a leg of mutton is cut, ought to be loudly execrated ; they must be taught to cut a scoop piece out of the knuckle end, and then go on from this, fat and lean together. It is the best and most economical method : if you can't do it, take a lesson from a ham and beef shop window, the first time you pass. You may be sure they know better about the matter than you do. A very polite and intelligent gentleman named Costerton sat next to me, and from him I derived much information. At Macao about four. The usual row and fighting with the boats. A-Tye amongst them, who recognized me with "Missa Smiss !—tluely my velly glad can see your facey ;" so on shore with her and up to Mr. William Dent's. In the evening called on Madame Bourbelon—a Scotch lady, and the wife of the French consul here. There was a charming leafy balcony, prettily lighted, leading from the Salon.

The mosquitoes at night rather worried me ; and being restless I walked out on the balcony. The sun had been so powerful during the day, that even now the heat of the tiled floor was uncomfortable to my naked feet.

Monday, 20*th*.—The mail arrived at Macao early this morning, so I caught a sight of the *Home News*. The *Willamette* left at 10, with a French priest on board, who had escaped the massacre at Siam. Into Hong-Kong harbour, at 2.30 ; with all the ships on the main-land side of the harbour expecting a typhoon. Up to the club, with a procession of eight coolies, carrying my effects ; and was very glad to find my old room available. Then to the P. and O. office, where I found all sorts of jolly letters from home, with the *Era* and *Daily Telegraph*, *en suite*. To dine quietly with Mr. Fischer and Mr. Sutherland, and then took all my papers and letters to bed, and read them until two.

This night, mosquitoes, cock-roaches, small red ants, "prickly heat," and a rat, kept me very lively.

Tuesday, 21st.—To breakfast with Mr. Alcock, meeting Mr. Carrol, just arrived on an appointment. Then to the police-court, where Mr. Tudor Davis was trying the very boy who picked my pocket, for a similar offence. Arranged with Mr. Mitchell about giving an entertainment next Saturday, for the charities; and then on board the *Sanspareil*, now down from the Bogue Forts, to see Captain Maguire. Next to the *Amethyst*, and to the *Calcutta*. Found a box from home, when I arrived, and it was a great treat to unpack it, as a few familiar things turned up. This is the worst day of "prickly heat" I have had.

Dined with Mr. Mitchell in the evening, with the acting Attorney-General, Mr. Green, with whom he shares the house. We had shark's-fin soup. Laughed and talked a great deal; but it was a sort of Chinese festival, and the people let off strings of crackers so continuously, that at times we could scarcely hear ourselves speak.

Poor Mr. Day, with whom I had dined at Mr. Bridges', died to-day at noon, and a circular came round about the funeral, which is to be at six o'clock to-morrow morning. There have been two or three very sudden deaths during my stay at Canton, including that of Dr. Harland, than whom no man was more beloved in the colony. They say here, if the wind had gone round to the N.E. these would not have occurred.

This evening the mountains were all hidden in a hot slate-coloured mist, and there was continuous lightning.

Wednesday, 22nd.—A wet, cool day—such a relief. Was at home packing, and got through a great deal of other work. Then to see Mr. May, at the Police. He told me the Chinese burglars like to bore through brickwork, rather than make a noise by destroying it; and when they make a hole in a wooden door, they put a lighted slow match in, which they keep blowing, to burn it larger.

Dined with Mr. Howe (Wardley and Co.) to-day. He has a large house, with some fine Swiss views framed in the corridor. Then to a concert at Mr. Lemann's in Almack's-place. It was admirably sustained by amateurs ; and the whole thing very well done.

Here is the programme:—

In consequence of Mr. Simonsen's departure for Shanghae the Programme has been necessarily varied.

PROGRAMME. PART FIRST.—1. Grand Sonata, Pianoforte—*Beethoven.* 2. Song Serenade—*Molique.* 3. Pianoforte, Duet. Between the Parts will be given a reminiscence of the celebrated Trial for Breach of Promise of Marriage, "BARDELL v. PICKWICK," with the Speeches of Counsel and Examination of the Witnesses.

PART SECOND.—1. Pianoforte, Solo. 2. Song, "Come into the garden, Maud"—*Balfe.* 3. Solo—Pianoforte—Fantasie on "Euryanthe"—*Thalberg.* 4. Pianoforte, Duet. In consequence of the length of the Programme the Concert will commence precisely at half-past eight.

Thursday, 23rd.—Again nice and cool. To breakfast with Colonel Caine, high up the hill, meeting Captains Brooker and Saumarez. The breakfast table was admirably laid out with bands of flowers and leaves of the parsley geranium, done by the native servants. Then up to the *China Mail* office, where Mr. Dixon offered to print the programmes of the entertainment for nothing, as it was for a charity. At noon went shopping with Mr. Lapraik, who was good enough to devote a great deal of his time to me this morning. We bought some very odd things, including a fan, which apparently fell all to pieces on turning the stick the wrong way. The rain has continued all day, and the thermometer has fallen to 78°. Dined with Mr. Tudor Davies— a small party, and some agreeable music.

Friday, 24th.—To breakfast with Mr. Alcock, and then back to pack, getting a little bewildered with all my affairs, as I have nobody who can help me. An old Chertsey fellow-townsman, Mr. Driver—on board one of the ships here—came to see me. At noon with four coolies and my luggage to the P. and O., holding a consultation with Mr. Fischer and Mr. Sutherland about their transit, and then in a chair to Mr. Jardine's, at East Point. I was fortunate enough to find him at home, and he promised me some seeds from his beautiful gardens. Then to Captain Twiss's, with my travelling tool-chest, to saw the handles off the spears he gave me. Next to Mr. Dent's, who promised to send me a man, learned in matting and rattan packing, to-morrow. Then to the *China Mail* office to correct the proofs of the programme—very well set up; and then to Mr. Green's, to try his piano, and arrange with Mr. Mitchell about the tickets, seats, &c. I next went to Lindsey's for some money, meeting young Mr. Antrobus, and then on board the *Sanspareil*, and had some soup with Captain Maguire and Captain Saumarez, which was very refreshing, for I was pretty well knocked up. When I came home I found that Mr. Dent had sent me a little chest of very fine tea, *Padre Oolong.* Got through more pigeon to-day than any other.

At seven Mr. Alcock called for me, and we walked together to the Parade landing, where Mr. Forth joined us; and then to dine with Sir Michael on board the *Calcutta.* We were fourteen in all. An admirable band played on deck during dinner; and the whole scene interested me very much. After dinner they chatted and smoked out on the gallery, from Hong Kong, which, lighted up, looked, as usual, uncommonly effective. Home by 11.

Saturday, 25th.—Early this morning, Mr. Martin, of the Police Court, came with the Chinese carpenters to put up my platform, in the Club Drawing-room, which they did in an uncommonly short space of time, making it, as they do everything, all of bamboo. Then two pianos arrived, one from Mr. Green, and another from Mr. Kingsmill, the latter of which I used. Captain Twiss and Mr. Chambers came to help me arrange the properties. It was quite like the old work in the assembly rooms and town-halls, when I used to travel with my "Overland Mail," and very refreshing. At noon, took my heavy luggage on board the *Sanspareil* to come round the Cape. Then, with Mr. Murray, to the P. and O., where I saw all my other things regularly put up and directed, thanks to Mr. Fischer and Mr. Suther- land. Sir John Dowring called, and we talked for a while. Pow, my small boy, when he brought me my shoes, said, "All right to-night, makee sing-song very good."

All the afternoon preparing, and at seven dined at the Club, with Captains McCleverty, Saumerez, and Brooker. The people began to come long before the time, and when I went into the room, it was choked full, even to the approaches and balconies. This was the programme:—

VICTORIA,  HONGKONG.

Programme

OF

Mr. Albert Smith's

ENTERTAINMENT,

CHIEFLY RELATING TO

THE TRAVELLING ENGLISH,

AND

THEIR AUTUMNAL PECULIARITIES

ON THE CONTINENT,

AS REPRESENTED FOR THE BENEFIT OF THE LOCAL CHARITIES,

IN THE DRAWING ROOM OF THE CLUB HOUSE, HONGKONG,

ON

SATURDAY EVENING,

THE 25th SEPTEMBER, 1858,

The Lecture will commence at Half-past Eight precisely, and occupy about two hours.

Price of Admission, Two Dollars-and-a-Half.

NOTICE. The Audience are respectfully but earnestly requested to be in their places by the time fixed for the commencement of the Lecture, which will be kept very punctually.

PART I.

OFF TO SWITZERLAND.

With a few words about the Old Diligence. The start by the South-Eastern Railway, *via* Dover, Calais, Lille, Malines, and Cologne, to the Rhine. Of BROWNE and his peculiarities abroad, especially his mistaken powers of illustration.

SONG, "THE YOUNG ENGLISH TRAVELLER."

THE RHINE,

Of the four Miss SIMMONDS's—ANNIE, who loves Tennyson so; FLORENCE, the fast; JANE, the neither-one-thing-nor-the-other; and BABY, the unpleasantly candid. Also, of Mr. PEABODY TAYLOR, an American Traveller; and of Mr. MUFF, a London Swell, who is bored.

SONG, THE "BELLE OF THE SALL."

ZURICH.

The Fair Time, and its wonders. The Showman's description of *Kasperl* (the German Punch), and his wonderful adventures. A Swiss Cheap Jack.

A NOVEL DESCRIPTION OF COURTSHIP.

END OF THE FIRST PART.

Between the Parts an Entr'Acte of a quarter of an hour, during which, some Gentlemen Amateurs, who have kindly given their assistance on this occasion, will perform some favourite Glees, &c.

PART II.

THE RIGI.

Of Mr. PARKER,—the unfortunate Gentleman, who never knew his own mind; and more especially of the PRANCER, and her influence on Society in England. Mr. Parker and the Prancer attempt a

DUET—CORNET A PISTON AND PIANO,

THE GREAT ST. BERNARD,

Of Mr. PRINGLE and His Great ST. BERNARD Dog. Also of his wonderful Photographs. Of Miss POTTLES, the Literary Prancer. Mr. HOWARD, the quick Traveller, and his

PATTER SONG, "BROWN ON HIS TRAVELS."

AT SEA,

The Story of the English Engineer, in the service of the Austrian Lloyd's Company.

PARIS,

The Troubles of an Englishman, who does not speak French very well, at a Restaurant in the Palais Royal.

SONG, "GALIGNANI'S MESSENGER."

I never had so good an audience, and literally everybody was there, from Sir John Bowring and Sir Michael Seymour downwards. Some of my attacks on the routine of conventional society appeared to startle them a little at first, and they looked at one another with that expression, which I know so well with my London morning audiences from the suburbs, of "Good gracious! what will he say next? Ought we to laugh at this, or not?" But I had evidently a few old Piccadilly friends in the room, to tell them it was all right and perfectly well received at this Hall ; and then, of course, they entered into it. The whole thing went off capitally ; and when I put a leader from one of the Hong Kong papers, about Sir Michael Seymour, into verse, and into *Galignani*, there was a roar of approbation that almost knocked me off my legs. When it was all over I had some ginger-beer and brandy down stairs at the bar, but the whole club was swarming with fellows, so I crept quietly off to bed; about eleven. We cleared £200 by the show, which was left with Mr. Tudor Davis and Mr. Mitchell, to distribute *à discrétion*.

Sunday, 26th.—To breakfast with Mr. Chambers, to talk over last night with Mr. Henry Dent and Mr. Scarth. Then went off fast asleep in the balcony on a bamboo chair, and when I awoke found myself all alone. To lunch with Mr. Bridges, meeting Mr. Caldwell, who told me the Cantonese reported that the "braves" were all disbanded—if so they would all turn pirates, and make it worse than ever. Mr. Bridges said that an Australian man had made an offer for all the hills about Hong Kong, now perfectly useless, to rear sheep upon, but that his offer had not been accepted. He also told me that the Chinese had made a great to do and met in the Temple about cutting through the spur of Victoria Peak to the west of Hong Kong, because they believe, when it is finished, the joss will send legions of white ants to eat up the city. The Bowring Praja, a waterside esplanade, is being finished towards the west, but there is great quarrelling about it. The resident English say, for the same sum of money that it will cost, Hong Kong could be permanently supplied with water, from the want of which, the common people, at times, suffer severely. To dine with Mr. Dent, meeting the Governor of Macao.

Monday, 27th.—To breakfast with Sir John Bowring, meeting Mr. Alcock and Mr. Caldwell, the "Protector of the Chinese." On board the *Norna*, in which, to my great comfort, I am to voyage again. She has been caught in a typhoon, and obliged to put into Amoy, since I left her. Occupied all day with packing my things for the return, and at 6.30 to dine with Mr. Caldwell, passing one of the most agreeable evenings with his family, that I had spent at Hong Kong. Mrs. Caldwell is Chinese, and the little children speak in the language. At ten I went out with him, armed, for a prowl about the low quarters, and saw a wonderful deal. [*Mem.:* This part of the diary is rather for private circulation than publicity.]

Tuesday, 28th.—Dr. Kenney, the oldest English practitioner at Hong Kong, called this morning, and gave me a beautiful pair of ladies' little shoes ; also a bit of the famous "poisoned bread," and some prettily carved bracelets. I much regret I did not make his acquaintance sooner. Then took my things on board the *Norna*, and went to get my passport *visée'd* for France. How cheering it looked—"*Bon pour*

D

se rendre en France par les paquebots Anglais de la malle!"
Mr. Lapraik kept up his attention to the last, going out with me for
my final shopping. Back to the club at one. And now I leave the
Hong Kong Daily Press to blow my trumpet as regards my departure.
I received it a fortnight after my arrival in England :—

"If the pleasure of pleasing, and the consciousness of having contributed
comfort to the poor and needy, can afford satisfaction to a Christian, Mr. Albert
Smith must leave China a happy man. It really was an act of great politeness
in him to afford this community the felicity of witnessing his powers of enter-
taining, and the managing of it in the manner he did, for the benefit of the
charities, evinced a noble feeling, and the sensitiveness of a true gentleman.
Had he given one entertainment for his own benefit towards defraying his
travelling expenses, and another for the benefit of the charities, he would still
have been entitled to great credit. Had he left without affording the community the pleasure of gratifying their curiosity in witnessing his far-famed powers,
he might have been deemed a little ill-natured. But to gratify the public—to
give alms to the poor—and take the consciousness of doing good, and the
applause of a community he will never see again, for his reward, was doing the
thing handsomely. We say, 'God bless him!'
"His success was unprecedentedly brilliant in the annals of China. The
rooms were thronged, the audience were in raptures; and although the admit-
tance was very low, the receipts exceeded £200 of clear profit.
"The Chinese were greatly puzzled what to make of Mr. Albert Smith. He
mixed with them as much as he possibly could, and tickled them amazingly
with his drollery. They saw he was a celebrity among his countrymen, and they
came to the conclusion that he was something between a sage and a funny devil.
When, however, they found that all the respectable foreigners in the colony
thronged to the entertainment he gave, and learnt that all the proceeds of the
same were given to the charities, they *ai-yaed* with astonishment and approbation. They seemed determined to give vent to their feelings in some way, and
they certainly hit upon a most effectual plan: for they paid him a compliment
that never was before accorded to any white mortal man.
"Accordingly, at the time appointed for Mr. Smith to leave the Club, a very
handsome sedan chair awaited him, with all the paraphernalia of a celestial
procession—music to drive away demons, and to call attention to the parade.
Flags with devices setting forth his virtues and talents. Emblems denoting
offerings and sacrifices for peace and plenty to be his lot on earth, with happiness
and fame afterwards. Thus conveyed and accompanied, he was carried through
the town down to the wharf of the P. and O. Company, where he embarked
amidst a display of fire crackers, which were meant to propitiate the elements
until he should be safely landed at home.
"Mr. Albert Smith has just cause to be proud of his reception in China, and
of the unique ovation made on his quitting it. He won the hearts of all here;
and was literally overwhelmed with presents in the shape of Chinese curios,
which money could not have bought, and for which the colony was ransacked to
throw at his feet. He must have received many things which cannot be
replaced, and we should say he has the means to furnish a museum which never
had its equal in Europe, and which George Robins would be at a stand-still to
puff up."

All this pleased me very much indeed, and I do not mind saying so.
To return to my diary. As I left the club, all the fellows gave me
a good English "Three times three." I could hardly fancy that it
was all real—that after all my trouble about a Chinese procession,
when I wrote *Aladdin* for the Lyceum, during the Keeley manage-

ment in 1844, I should become the hero of one myself—that I should be going in state to court Miss Woolgar with Mr. Wigan for my rival, and Mr. Frank Mathews for my father-in-law, as *my* Aladdin had done. All the balconies at Lane and Crawfurd's, the Commercial Hotel, Mrs. Marsh's Millinery Rooms, &c., were crowded with people, and my heart was up in my mouth all the time. When we got to the P. and O. office, I met Mr. Fisher, Mr. Sutherland, Captain Rogers, Captain Brooks, Mr. George Lyall, and more friends; but the people carried me right down to the wharf before they put me down. Then into the balcony for a sea-horse "stirrup cup;" and at two on board the *Norna*, where my last present was a handsome female costume from Lieut. Cardale. Hearty wishes and a warm parting on all sides. Here is our party from *The Daily Press* of to-day :—

"Per *Norna*, str., to sail to-day at 2 P.M.

"*For Southampton.*—Captain Jenkins, R.N., Lieutenant Brent R.N., Mrs. Mottley, Mr. Thos. Abbott, Mr. Aspinall, Lieutenant E. Madden, R.N., Rev. E. H. Robinson, Mr. T. Oldknow, and Lieut. Travers.

"*For Marseilles.*—Messrs. Albert Smith, Loch, A. Meynard, P. Flottard, T. K. Holdsworth, and William Dent.

"*For Malta.*—Mr. R. Pearce.

"*For Alexandria.*—H. E. Count Poutiatine, Baron d'Osten-Sacken, and Mr. Peschouroff.

"*For Pont de Galle.*—Mr. Cave, and Mr. Wm. Bane."

The feeling that my object is over: and that I am going home again, is very strange—but uncommonly pleasant. We went up nearly to East Point, round the *Calcutta*, and then back again to the western entrance of the harbour, and out into the sea. And as evening came on, the coast gradually faded away in the sunset. Good night to China!

APPENDIX.

Very little occurred between Hong Kong and Galle, in the *Norna*, on our way home, and my "log" was of the barest description. But to keep up the accurate progress of days, in order to register our voyage correctly, I will copy them.

Wednesday, September 29th.—Mr. Loch, who was carrying home the Japan treaty, lost one of the curious little spaniels, which he had brought from Jeddo—evidently the germ of the King Charles' breed. The little thing had been left in his berth, and jumped through the port-hole into the sea. Michaelmas day, so we had goose for dinner.

Thursday, 30th.—Terrible storm of rain, thunder, and lightning.

Friday, October 1st.—The rain and wind continued so heavily, that I could not sleep on deck.

Saturday 2nd.—Fine and sultry. All eating, drinking, reading, and dozing.

Sunday, 3rd.—The Rev. Mr. Robinson, the military chaplain, who was also in the Crimea, preached. Saw a large ship at night.

Monday, 4th.—Dead calm, and doubts about catching the Indian boat at Galle. The sea was like blue glass at night, reflecting the stars. A fine comet to the west, which some of them had seen at Shanghae. The wind rose at night, and I rigged a wooden windsail outside my port, which turned the breeze well into my cabin.

Tuesday, 5th.—About six we met H.M.S. *Niger ;* she signalled to us to stop, and sent a boat on board ; but it was all nonsense—only to ask what news at Shanghae. At night it was really cold.

Wednesday, 6th.—Into the new harbour of Singapore at seven in the morning. To breakfast with Captain Marshall, who gave me all my letters and papers from home, which had been there some days. Then to call on a few friends, and about the town. It was very hot, and the prickly heat, which had left me for some few days, all came out again. To dine at Captain Marshall's with Captain Rogers and Mr. Whampoa. Saw plenty of English papers, with *Punch, Household Words*, and *Illustrated Times*, which is getting about well.

Thursday, 7th.—Still in Singapore. Called on Mr. Whampoa, who gave me some curious Chinese things, including a little box of edible bird's-nests. Called on Mr. Purves, who was also very kind, presenting me with specimens of Straits produce, and preparations of the nutmeg in all its different stages : also twenty or thirty small figures of Chinese actors excellently modelled. Mr. Little, in Commercial-square, gave me two shields. A great many people to see us off at the new harbour. We left with three cheers, and another for me, with which I was well pleased. The young Rajah of Queedah was on board—he was Europian in complexion, and excessively like Mr. Sims Reeves in face and figure.

Friday, 8*th.*—Nice breeze up the Straits. A lady, member of the Equestrian Circus at Batavia, joined us. She was Dutch, but spoke English, German, and French equally well : and we had a long talk about the different companies and their lady riders, especially Kate Cooke, Katchen Renz, Caroline, the Tourniares, and Palmyre Anato, all of whom she knew : which mightily confused the listeners, who at last gave it up as an unsatisfactory employment, and retired.

Saturday, 9*th.*—At Penang, at 10 A.M. : and up to breakfast at Mr. Padday's, meeting an old London friend, Mr. Underdown. About the town and bazaar for a stroll with Mr. Dent. On board again at 3, where we bought perfect bundles of Malacca canes, and 'Penang Lawyers'—sixpence each.

Sunday, 10*th.*—A dead calm, but they say we shall catch it, when we get out of the Straits.

Monday, 11*th.*—They were right. The S.W. monsoon well against us, and the passengers seedy and quiet.

Tuesday, 12*th.*—Head wind still, and the *Norna* labouring heavily. At night Dr. Slorach, Captain Jenkins, and one or two others, were all shot off their chairs at once, by a lurch.

Wednesday, 13*th.*—Finer weather, but going very slowly, not making seven knots. The luggage all got up to-day—weighed and charged for the Desert transit, which the purser is answerable for.

Thursday, 14*th.*—Wind ahead : one or two of the passengers have not appeared since Tuesday.

Friday, 15*th.*—Pitching continues. At night Mr. Soy got his drum and fiddle band into action, and there was a mad attempt at dancing, but I have seen a greater success on a steady floor.

Saturday, 16*th.*—Increased doubts about catching the *Alma* at Galle. At noon we had 113 miles to make, and 51 current=164. We had a little "sing-song pigeon" at night, and subscribed for a silver tea-service for Captain Rogers, on which occasion I had to make him a speech. We had kept the list confined to the English passengers, not thinking it fair to ask the foreigners, as it was almost a personal matter, but Admiral Poutiatine and M. Osten-Sacken insisted on sub-scribing.

Sunday, 17*th.*—Everybody anxious about the mail. Mr. Fleetwood says the coals will last, but about as much as they will. At half-past twelve at night—everybody up and on the look out—we sighted the Galle light. Sent up rockets and burnt blue lights—no response. About two, signalled again, when in five minutes, we were answered from the harbour. Great joy !

Monday, 18*th.*—Into Galle at 7 ; and Captain Rogers brought me my letters and papers, with a portrait and memoir of myself in the *Illustrated News of the World,* and a proof of my Willow-pattern Plate bill out from London. To breakfast with Mr. Logan, at the Bank ; then on board the *Alma* to see about my cabin, and look at the people ; and then up with the jingle to lunch with Captain Bayley and Mr. Sparkes, at their bungalow. The lovely and teeming tropical vegetation cannot be conceived. My friends had a charming little place, well stocked with poultry and all sorts of edible produce. Also, a porcupine in a cage, sharing it with Jacko, who kept well away from his quills : and a remarkably fine St. Bernard dog—a rare thing to see in the tropics.

On board the *Alma* at 4.30, and off at 6, cheering the *Norna* as we passed. The India passengers appear inclined to look down upon all our China party as intruders: and we are not going to have it. I have a nice cabin, high and roomy, but being to the fore, and the sea high, I am obliged to keep the port closed.

Tuesday, 19*th.*—Wind dead a-head, but doing nine knots. Captain Henry attentive to everybody, and Mr. Davis, the first officer, a right good fellow, whose kindness and companionable qualities greatly relieved the tedium of the Sea of Arabia. Was glad to find Mr. Hope with us—the engineer during the break-down of the *Bentinck.* All the people are in "sets;" as I hear all the Anglo-Indians usually are. We Celestials are determined not to have this—not caring one straw for these unknown Calcutta *cliques*—but to go well amongst them—mentally knock all their heads together, and make them agreeable to each other. One of the handsomest and most lady-like women on board, was all but cut, because she was not in a "set." Snobbery appears, like weeds, to spring up to an enormous size in the Presidencies.

Wednesday, 20*th.*—To-night the stewards, and superior part of the crew, had a musical meeting at the fore. They sang some glees very well. I joined them, and took my share in the performances with pleasure.

Thursday, 21*st.*—Rain to-day. People gradually forming into philandering couples. Some singing to the piano in the saloon. Was glad to meet a son of Mr. Macready, on board, with his lady. He is in delicate health, and is going to Madeira. It was truly refreshing to talk about several mutual London friends with him. All the cabin ports open at night, and nice and cool. Never saw so many odd and varied styles of all sorts of chairs, as the people have on deck. Am very proud of my own, which Mr. Fisher gave me at Hong Kong. It is out and away the best.

Saturday, 23*rd.*—Cloudy and cool. Saw shoals of flying-fish all day long. Invented a ballet and a scene for Beverley in the sunset clouds, which were, for a while, very beautiful. Lovely evening, and a wonderful moon, so clear that I am writing this in pencil.

Sunday, 24*th.*—Rows amongst the women—of course. How terribly and uncharitably spiteful women are about one another—if in some of their brighter attributes they approach much nearer than men to the angel, in one or two other respects they certainly come closer to the other party. In the main, however, the Indians and the Chinese are amalgamating very satisfactorily.

Monday, 25*th.*—Some of the ladies and young officers have requested the chaplain to read prayers every morning in the saloon; and they all go there. Some wretchedly ribald minds have christened the meeting the Agapemone. Holding myself honestly to be neither better nor worse than the rest of the world, I *always* mistrust a display of religion.

Tuesday, 26*th.*—Passed Socotra in the night, and off the African coast in the morning. The weather continued cool and fine, and we have agreeable little meetings on the forecastle at night, for songs, stories, and conversation.

Wednesday, 27*th.*—Once more approaching the terrible Red Sea, and the temperature is already rising. Into Aden at 6.30 P.M. Up to Mr. Thomas's, and found all my next batch of letters and newspapers—in fact I supply the whole ship with literature. Mr. Dent and I availed ourselves of Mr. Thomas's hospitality, and slept, whilst the *Alma* coaled, on two sofas, in the corridor of his bungalow.

Thursday, 28th.—Dined at Mr. Thomas's, and was charmed to meet my old fellow-traveller, the Rev. Mr. Badger, at dinner. He is greatly interested in the Red Sea Telegraph: and told me all that had happened at Djedda, since we parted. The talking bird was in good health, and more conversational than ever. On board at eight, and "signed the coal warrants" in Captain Henry's cabin.

Friday, 29th.—Going up the Red Sea at 14 knots an hour, with the wind aft, after passing Mocha. Heat increasing. Mr. Abbott (who is very ill, and occupies my chair) and I get together every evening to talk about home and drink tea—very different from the run of my London life.

Saturday, 30th.—Read "Jane Eyre" again, and found it as unpleasantly powerful as ever. In the evening we had a charming little musical party of five, at the stern of the boat, behind the cabins.

Sunday, 31st.—Dreadfully hot, and I am grieved to say, several of the audience, at church, went off fast asleep during the sermon. At night a heavy mist and dew, and the thermometer at 88°.

Monday, November 1st.—Much cooler this morning. At night—the last on board the *Alma*—I gave a sing-song pigeon. Mr. Davis fitted up the deck very effectively, and I repeated my Hong-Kong programme. Gave the proceeds, through Mr. Robinson, to a poor woman on board, with her three grandchildren, whose father had been killed at Lucknow. The very decent poverty of this little family commanded general sympathy.

Tuesday, 2nd.—Packing for the Desert all the morning. Got to Suez at 2.30 P.M., and on shore with Lieutenant Blakeley, the Admiralty Agent, and Mr. Loch, with his remaining little Japan spaniel "Fusey" —so called after Fuseyama, the sacred mountain of Japan. Slept at the Hotel at Suez. Not very hot, but the flies and mosquitoes beyond endurance. All felt very jolly at being "so near home"—so near home! at Suez. One of the usual Arab rows in the middle of the night, which I always hear of in Egypt. The water for washing so swarmed with tadpoles and horrors, that I was obliged to strain it through the mosquito curtains before I could use it.

Wednesday, 3rd.—Up at 7, and did some button-pigeon with my 'hussef'. Still cooler. The rest of the *Alma* people came on shore after breakfast, and we started across the Desert, in the vans, at 11. In an hour and a-half we reached the railway terminus.* Waited here, with the usual nasty refreshment, for an hour and a-half, and then, going full speed, reached Cairo at 4, meeting the outward mail. Amongst the passengers was Mr. Henry Spicer, the manager of the old Olympic Theatre. We did not leave the terminus, but quitted Cairo again at 5, and got to Alexandria, at half past 1 in the morning, all pretty well knocked up. The hotel taken by storm—Tortillia's, formerly Rey's—and Lieutenant Travers and I were fortunate enough to get a good double-bedded room.

---

* The line is now open throughout, from Alexandria to Cairo and Suez.

Thursday, 4th.—Noise as usual in the night, with the addition of—I should think—thousands of dogs, cats, and cocks. To the P. and O. office in the square, where I found bundles of letters from home, and newspapers. At noon on board the *Euxine*, Captain Roberts, for Marseilles, starting in half-an-hour. The *Ceylon* left after us, but was soon a-head and out of sight at night. We are very few on board—not above ten or twelve : so much the better. Very tired, and went to bed at nine.

Friday, 5th.—All very dull : but the thermometer is down to 76° : and we are nearing home. A cough.

Saturday, 6th.—The deck is quite deserted, and my cough is very bad, so I have routed out a cloth coat, and put on a waistcoat. Great arguments and surmises all day about the quarantine at Marseilles. Nobody knows anything about it.

Sunday, 7th.—Heavy rain and squall at day-break : and very cold on deck—a new and strange sensation. Muster of crew, before church : and it was odd to hear them all answer in English again. At noon saw the *Panther*, outward bound, on the horizon, and got into Malta at nine in the evening, with rockets and blue lights. Went on shore with Mr. Denham, the purser, and some other gentlemen. First to the P. and O. agents, and then to telegraph to London that I had reached Malta all right. Presently we met Mr. Pearce, one of our old *Alma* party, so we all went to Durnford's hotel, for supper and champagne. Then bought some mittens and coral in a neighbouring shop, and back to the *Euxine* at midnight. Slept well, through the awful row of coaling all night long.

Monday, 8th.—Sicily on our right, on coming on deck this morning. Very cold : a dull wintry sky : rain : and no awning. Kept in my cabin nearly all day, sketching out my entertainment, writing, dozing, and — washing my pocket handkerchiefs ! It was all so lamentably stupid, on board, that I went to bed at 8.30.

Tuesday, 9th.—Caught sight of Sardinia after breakfast. It is so strange to see the people all wrapped up, shivering about, and getting into the sun to warm. There is a dull old Captain on board who wears us to death, by playing tunes badly, with one finger, on the piano. To bed, as usual, before nine.

Wednesday, 10th.—Passed the Strait of Bonifacio in the night, and awoke at 3.30 by the boat rolling heavily. I was so shot backwards and forwards in my berth, that I got a bad headache, and my cough distressed me very much. The sea very rough all day, and I was twice thrown off my sofa. A perpetual noise of crockery being knocked about and broken, and dinner a matter of great difficulty. Sighted the French coast about 7 P.M. when the sea fell. Off Marseilles about ten, when we lay to, and it was tolerably calm.

Thursday, 11th.—Into Marseilles harbour at seven in the morning. Captain Roberts and the Doctor went on shore, and found we were in quarantine. They brought me some more letters and papers. We then went back to the quarantine ground at Frieul, near the Chateau d'If, which is little more than a desolate quarry. Landed and walked over the island, which has some very picturesque irregular bays—charming for bathing. Watched some fishermen, who caught sardines in a long net; and strolled about to read all my letters again. Then to see some blasting in the quarry ; and somehow or another, the day passed pretty quickly.

Friday, 12*th.*—The health officer and a Mossoo doctor came on board about 12 and gave us pratique. To the *Hotel des Colonies*, which I recommend to travellers, as far more comfortable than the *Ambassadeurs*, or the *Empereurs.* How pleasant it was to be at Marseilles again ! Strolled about the town in all the delight of civilisation, and sent a telegram home. At 10 P.M. to the railway, meeting Mr. Loch. Started at 10.30., and the night terribly cold.

Saturday, 13*th.*—Ice everywhere in the morning, and all the way up to Paris. The dinner at Dijon not so good as usual. Reached Paris at 6.30 P.M. and at once to the Calais railway, with not too much time to do it. At Calais at three in the morning, and a very rough passage over.

Sunday, 14*th.*—Stepped on shore in England at 5 A.M., and to the Lord Warden, where I enjoyed my English breakfast tremendously, with Mr. Loch and "Fusey"—my only companions, all the way, from China. Reached London Bridge at 11, and

H O M E !

TEA LEAVES.

AN APPENDIX OF WHIMS AND WAIFS OF THE JOURNEY, WHICH MAY BE
READ OR NOT ACCORDING TO THE TASTE OF THE READER.

SHEPHEARD'S, AT CAIRO.

Shepheard's Hotel at Cairo is where the travellers by the Overland
Mail usually stop. There is a story told of an old lady who went to
France to write a book about it; and the first night she arrived at
Calais she put down her impressions in her journal, to the effect "that
if it had not been for the sea passage, and the difference of the
language, and in fact the totally different appearance of everything
altogether, she should not have known she had been out of England."
This description will not apply to Shepheard's Hotel; the difficulty
there is, under any circumstances, to believe you are away from home.
The rooms are fitted up entirely in the English style; with the latest
London prints, the latest number of *Punch*, and the *Illustrated London
News* are on the side tables. The dinner-service bears the imprint of
the Potteries; the cutlery is all marked with some well-known Shef-
field or London name; and I believe if you were to speak any other
language than English to the Arab attendants they would not understand you. But with all this, the Hotel has a very uncertain patron-
age. Sometimes there are only two people there for a few days—
these are simply tourists who are going up the Nile—and then the
mail arrives, and a hundred people come in all at once, and each
insists upon having a separate bed, and a very large bed-room. And
when it chances that the outward mail meets the one coming home,
then the Spread Eagle at Epsom, the night before the Derby, if they
were going, from some turf convulsion, to run the St. Leger the same
day, would be comparatively quiet to it.

THE NILE BOAT.

BALLAD.

[Written by BROWN, when he had done 'the thing to do' and got up to Philœ,
above the first Cataract, without experiencing any great excitement. To the air of
"Hunting the Hare."]

Travelling Authors who poke their jokes odd at us
　　Giving full play to their Pegasus' wings,
Going from Warburton back to Herodotus,
　　Writing of Egypt, tell wonderful things.
　　　　Naught can be rarer,
　　　　Or brighter or fairer,
Or grander, whate'er a man's passion or style.
　　　　But if it don't bore ye,
　　　　In plain honest story,
I'll tell you the joys of a Boat on the Nile.

A dozen dark Arabs compose the wild crew of it—
  Scantily dressed, in fact, scarcely at all;
No one would trust himself, not if he knew of it,
  With such a set in the dark or a squall;
      Screaming and fighting,
      And kicking and biting,
    And terror exciting for mile after mile;
      Your pleasure all barter'd,
      You look to be martyr'd,
  And wish you'd ne'er chartered your Boat on the Nile.

The Kandjia itself is of wood, and unpainted,
  And swarms with a legion of horrible things;
Especially rats—at which tourists have fainted—
  And little musquitoes with very large stings.
      Tired of keeping
      Awake, you try sleeping,
    And time slowly creeping you think to beguile;
      When a horrid large race
      Of big spiders give chase,
  And run over your face in your Boat on the Nile.

All along you see nothing but villages,
  Peopled by savages, pigeons, and sheep,
Excepting the Pasha some wretched place pillages,
  Leaving it only a mighty dust heap.
      If the wind's falling,
      Your Kandjia is crawling,
    And Arabs are hauling an hour a mile:
      With heat all is hazy.
      Ennuyé and lazy,
  It drives you half crazy, your Boat on the Nile.

Human life leaving, no letters receiving,
  Having no notion of things that have passed—
Perhaps some Nile ranger you meet as a stranger,
  May lend you *The Times* of the month before last.
      But what's our metropolis,
      Near Heliopolis;
    Who cares for London, near Carnac's old pile?
      Midst old mummies rotten,
      Your friends are forgotten,
  And so may you be in your Boat on the Nile.

Bored to death by the want of variety,
  Wishing some steamer could take you in tow;
Feeding on chickens and eggs to satiety,
  Eating tough bread that is made more like dough.
      By heat overpowered,
      By small flies devoured,
    Your temper quite soured, you never can smile;
      And though it may cook
      Up a very good book,
  For pleasure don't look in a Boat on the Nile!

THE CAIRO DONKEYS.

Donkey-riding in Cairo is a very exciting sport, not to be conceived by those whose experience ends in England. It requires a combination of various attributes—great physical powers, an undaunted spirit of enterprise, an indurated heart, a general absence of pride, stout lungs, no end of a whip, and great disregard of the Prophet. When you have made up your mind to go abroad in the streets, you come down to the steps of Shepheard's Hotel, and as soon as you are seen, every donkey-boy below the acacias opposite makes a charge at you. There is small difference between the boys of Cairo and the boys of Ramsgate. Little tawny Hassan, going to the Pyramids, with his faded skullcap, blue night-gown, and iron legs, shouts as lustily, whacks as unceasingly, runs as untiringly, and deports himself generally as saucily as Bill Simmons, on the road to Pegwell Bay or the North Foreland. At the first charge, by which you are at once driven back into the Court of the hotel, Shepheard comes to the rescue. He runs out armed with a wiry bit of rope, with which he licks them (it is the best word) about the head and face and legs. They retreat in great confusion ; and you take courage and advance. But you have scarcely emerged from the gateway when another rush is made. This time, however, they make shields of their donkeys, seizing them by the heads and backing them against you, the animals forming such a defence that the boys are beyond the reach of Shepheard's rope. But there is sure to be a dragoman loitering about the hotel, who attacks the enemy in the rear with a *kurbash*—a whip of buffalo-hide,—and another wild retreat takes place. Then you choose one donkey, and whilst the driver is beating back his rivals he neglects to hold the stirrup-leather, and you come to the ground the instant you attempt to mount ; for the reason that the stirrups on the Cairo donkey-saddles are not each hung separately, as with us, but attached to two ends of a strap, which passes over the seat, so that you can see-saw your legs, up and down, as you will. At last you are fairly in your seat, with a large round pommel before you, as big as a quartern loaf, and, with a wild yell, the boy starts the donkey off at a gallop along the Esbekeyah.

CROSSING THE DESERT.
(A REMINISCENCE OF 1849.)
THE   CAMEL   RIDE.
AIR.—*"I remember."*

I remember, I remember,
  How the babies flitted by,
To be packed up last December,
  In the desert four-horse fly.
I remember, from those criers,
  What an awful noise arose,
With the screaming of those Ayahs,
  Who were all as black as crows.
I remember, I remember,
  How mosquitoes flitted by,
And though it was December,
  It was much more like July !

I remember, I remember,
 How I peeped into that van,
And I said, "With those small parties,
 Go I'm sure I never can ;"
So I thought the route to vary,
 I would try and have a ride,
And they brought a dromedary
 That I rashly got outside.
I remember, I remember,
 It was anything but fun,
And I wish'd that hot December
 All my desert sand was run.

For I only had a slight rope,
 That tremendous brute to guide,
And I felt upon a tight rope,
 With a stitch in either side.
With his speed the still wind blew hard,
 And he shied, and sometimes knelt,
And I longed to call out "Steward,"
 For so very ill I felt.
And I got so hot and jolted,
 I could only gasp and cough,
And at Cairo's gates he bolted,
 And at last he pitched me off.
I remember, I remember,
 That for worlds I would not try,
From that sample in December
 What it must be in July.

———

BILL OF FARE.

OF A DINNER ON BOARD A PENINSULAR AND ORIENTAL STEAMER
(BETWEEN SUEZ AND GALLE).

S. S. "Alma," Octr. 22nd, 1858.

MOCK TURTLE SOUP.
ROAST FORE QUARTER MUTTON.
ROAST QUARTER PORK.
BOILED LEG MUTTON.
SUCKING PIG.
ROAST GOOSE.
ROAST DUCKS.
CORNED PORK AND PEAS PUDDING.
PIGEON PIES.
MUTTON CUTLETS.
ROAST CAPONS.
PILLAU OF FOWLS.
HAM.
ROAST FOWLS.
ROAST HAUNCH MUTTON.
COMPOTE DE PIGEON.
GIBLET PIES.
BOILED FOWLS.
PORK A L'ITALIEN.
BRAISED RIBS MUTTON.
PIGS FEET RAGOUT.
SAVOURY PATTIES.
CURRY AND RICE.

SECOND COURSE.

MARMALADE PUDDING.
BREAD AND BUTTER PUDDING.
BANBURY CAKES.
JAM PATTIES.
CHERRY TARTS.
DAMSON TARTS.
FANCY PASTRY.
BOTTLED PALE ALE.
BOTTLED STOUT.
PORT.
SHERRY.
CLARET.
MADEIRA.

AN UNEXPECTED BORE.

" Are you going to Shanghae, Mr. Smith ?"
" I said, ' No—why ? ' "
" Oh ! you must go to Shanghae. *Why* don't you go to Shanghae ?"
" I never thought about it. What is there to see there ?"
" Oh ! there are some very nice people there."
" And such beautiful silk !"
" And an excellent mission.   It's a very interesting station."
And then they all chorused, " Ah ! you *must* go to Shanghae."
This conversation took place one day between Mr. Blandy, Florence,
Baby Simmonds, and myself, as we were standing under the portico of
a very charming bungalow, high up on the hill above Hong Kong.
While we were talking, Mr. Tonks, a tea-taster in ———'s house,
came on a little business, and said to me—
" Well, how are you by this time, Mr. Smith ?   Have you seen
much while you have been here ?"
" Oh ! an immense deal—I am delighted !"
" Ah, you should go to Shanghae to see things."
" There ! we told you so !" all the others broke out.
" But what is there to see there ?"
" Well, Shanghae's a curious place, Mr. Smith.   You see it *is* Hong
Kong, and yet it isn't, as you may say, according to how you look at
it.   I've seen as many as—oh ! I don't know how many English
walking on the Bund at night.   There's some capital houses there."
" Chinese ?"
" No, English—first-rate."
I had been worried a great deal already about all the commercial
houses, and I never once could make the different people understand
that I knew little, and cared less, about commercial China.   " Then
what had I come for ?" they would ask. They were always wondering,
what I could see in the China parts of Hong Kong, and recom-
mending me *always* to go to Shanghae, until I got actually angry at
their comprehending my object so much better than I did.   We have
all an innate dislike to be recommended to do anything.   When a club
fogey, for instance, points you out " something worth reading" in the
paper—ten to one but that is the only part you skip.
Besides, I had been before recommended by all to go to Macao : "just
the place for me," as they said.   I went, and found Macao, looking as
if a fifth-rate bit of Portugal had been caught up by a waterspout and

dropped down here by mistake, with nothing to recommend it but the beauty of the boat-girls. And they were very pretty—"*No.* 1 *handsome facee.*"

With all this, nobody could pitch upon one absolutely interesting feature at Shanghae. I got irritated—and I felt wrongly—with my best and kindest friends.

Mr. Dent was always impressing on me the necessity of going to Shanghae.

All the ladies, especially, said, "Oh! Mr. Smith, you must go to Shanghae."

Captain Rogers, of the *Norna*, said, "I am going up to Shanghae, Mr. Smith, I suppose I'm to keep your old cabin; you *may* see a typhoon."

And last of all, there was not one single clerk, or tea-taster, or manager, or principal, who did not say, "Why don't you go to Shanghae?"

I got in such a rage, that nothing on earth would have induced me to go. And this little song eventually stopped them.

WHY DON'T YOU GO TO SHANGHAE?

AIR.—"*The Low Backed Car.*"

When first I went to China,
  Some two or three months ago,
No weather could be finer,
  No spirits in better flow.
To see the heart of Canton
  I meant alone to try,
But, o'er and o'er, each stupid bore,
  Said "Why don't you go to Shanghae?"
Oh! you must go to Shanghae,
For China is all Shanghae,
  But wanting to know,
  Why they all said so,
None could tell me the reason why.

For strange as it may seem here,
  Our ignorance to own,
Shanghae's a place, to our West-end race,
  That's totally unknown.
But it lights a link—how strange to think,
  In whatever place confined,
That place is the world, if the truth is unfurled,
  To the pure commercial mind,
As it thinks of the silk of Shanghae,
And what English shops will buy—
  And the tourist is taught,
  All his work goes for naught
Unless he has been to Shanghae.

From what I can hear, it does appear
  The country's a perfect flat,
With no roads nor pikes—but canals and dykes—
  Well—there isn't much in that!
Besides, it takes five days to go,
  And five days to return,

And you meet the monsoon
And catch a typhoon,
   And find there is nothing to learn,
To make up for time lost at Shanghae.
Then *why* should folks ask me, " Why
   Since to China you've come,
   Before you go home,
Why don't you go to Shanghae ?

The China of which *we* want to learn
   Has little to do with trade,
Or markets or price, or godowns or rice,
   Or dollars in commerce made.
We want the land of pagodas grand,
   Of that old mysterious race,
Where print was shown,
And the compass known,
   E'er England raised her face.
And nobody'd heard of Shanghae
Till some stray ships passing by,
   Help'd to raise up a fund,
   To build up a Bund,
Where the poor devils walk at Shanghae.

If time turned round, it would be found,
   (May that chance ne'er arrive,)
Though Dent were dead, and Jardine had fled,
   Yet China would still survive.
Besides, we know, at a poultry show,
   Where cocks and hens outcry,
That the very tall, amongst them all
   Are called by the name of Shanghae.
But they *don't* come from Shanghae,
Nor from any Chinese place by—
   The country to buy 'em
   You'll find nearer Siam,
A very long way from Shanghae,

My journey o'er, to England's shore
   I'm bound, and wish to try,
To let London know, what China can show
   Without having been to Shanghae.
Its customs of yore, and its ancient lore,
   For what can that mind be,
Whose Chinese tone is confined alone,
   To Opium, Silk and Tea,
Or whatever they sell at Shanghae ?
And when I may happen to die,
   One favour I crave,
   That they'll put on my grave,
That *I* never went to Shanghae !

OF INDIAN SNOBS.

Sometimes I meet people who irritate me very much, and I wish it was allowable, in polite society, to throw something at their heads ; but I was most made so continuously angry by a lot of people I met coming home from India in one of the Peninsular and Oriental boats. You would have thought that India was the world, and England some small province, somewhere or another, used for brewing beer and preserving provisions. You would also have encountered the originals of those irritable old men in bygone five-act comedies, who swear, and bawl, and get red in the face, and talk emphasized trash all on one subject ; and you would have seen really nice women, originally, who had become so eaten up by a sense of some position or another, which gave them a poor little Calcutta precedence over one or two other ladies, that they would fidget and fuss and sulk for a week if they did not get the place at dinner that their station in the perspiring society of India afforded them.

The manner of all these people towards the servants of the ship was most atrocious. They looked upon them as so many niggers, to be driven and ordered about as occasion required ; and not a word of civility or acknowledgment ever passed their lips towards their inferiors. They were all helplessly, hopelessly, idle ; and could not even move a cushion from one chair to another without calling their "Boy !" whom they would afterwards keep tugging the punkahs for hours, until his arms must have been ready to drop off. But it was pleasant to know what rough checks all their whims would receive when they got to London. How they would be pushed about in the streets like any other average persons. How, in society, nobody would care one husk of a straw what they had been in Calcutta, unless they proved nice intelligent, agreeable persons in London. How those long-boring stories would be yawned down, and those imported sixth-hand anecdotes coldly crushed. How, above all, if they wanted anything done, they would be compelled to be commonly civil to our attentive household servants—even in the Brompton lodging, for which they had exchanged their big, bare, barn of a bungalow.

Very frequently we got up little concerts at night, on board the ship; and to teach those Anglo-Indians that they were not such wonders, I wrote the following lyrical lesson—

GREAT FAILURE IN THE EAST.

" There's nae luck."

There is a land, a long way off,
 Six thousand miles at least,
At which none yet have dared to scoff,
 'Tis called " The gorgeous East."
Its gems, its spice, its woods we praise,
 Its wealth—its native race—
But just the coat of tinsel raise,
 And 'tis a wretched place !
 Sing *Lalleballoo and jaggerbedam,*
  Sing *Pukkera dobie pore,*
 Sing *Cursejee, dirtyjee, jabberjehoy,*
  Sing *Chilly go wallah badore !**

---

* This chorus is pure Hindustani, but the Author is not allowed to publish its meaning.

E

Obedient to the tropic laws,
  The sun's a perfect lens,
Which cholera, plague, and fever draws
  From jungle, quags, and fens.
All day you gasp—all night you pant,
  And sweltering vigils keep,
Lest poisonous gnat, or stinging ant,
  Should through your curtains creep.
      Sing *Lalleballoo, &c.*

Your house a *bungalow* is called,
  O'er whose gaunt space you roam :
Its general tone is bare and bald—
  So unlike English home !
There are no bells, so if you want
  Your servant—"*Boy !*" you call;
When p'rhaps he comes; and if he don't,
  You still must sit and bawl.
    · Sing *Lalleballoo, &c.*

These servants you will always find,
  Not overclean, or sweet,
With tawdry rags about them twined,
  And fancy !—naked feet.
Ungrateful, idle, silent, sly,—
  Though humble they appear,
The dark expression of each eye,
  Is hatred quenched in fear.
      Sing *Lalleballoo, &c.*

The cookery is all dabby mess,
  Though meant to copy home :
For all is stale, you must confess,
  Which round the Cape has come.
The meats, preserved in air-tight pot,
  Oft go off with a bang !
And at the best, have always got
  A most suspicious twang.
      Sing *Lalleballoo, &c.*

The beef and mutton's all so tough—
  You cannot hang your meat,
You kill of what you want enough,
  That very day to eat !
But odds and ends you can re-dress,
  To make a " curry" nice,
And get so sick'ned of that mess,
  In its eternal rice.
      Sing *Lalleballoo, &c.*

The scorpion swarms about the house,
  The serpent—four feet long,—
The spider, cockroach, rat, and mouse,
  About the bedroom throng.
You eat ants wholesale—white and red—
  Or drink them in your tea,
And often, wriggling in your bread,
  A centipede you see !
      Sing *Lalleballoo, &c.*

You order all in tones severe,
　Half bullying, most absurd,
And " If you please," and " Thank you" here
　Are phrases never heard,
Its " Bitters !" " Water !" " Pepper !" " Tea !"
　But vengeance will come yet !
Just try that line at home and see
　What answers you will get.
　　　Sing *Lalleballoo, &c.*

You live in such a ring, confined
　To one small paltry state,
That for good general talk, your mind
　Grows perfectly stagnate.
When strangers come, you do not call
　On them—you're too great nobs :—
Which, by our *English* standard, seems
　Uncommonly like snobs !
　　　Sing *Lalleballoo, &c.*

And then your half-penny pretence,
　That shrouds your lack of wit,
Of ball or dinner "precedence,"
　And where you are to sit.
Oh ! Darling Snobs ! take my advice,
　And ne'er in England try,—
Even, if very *very* nice,
　Such ultra—flunkery.
　　　Sing *Lalleballoo, &c.*

And worst of all, each steamer brings
　Some lovely English girls,
Here to be sold, for wedding rings,
　To Chutney-livered churls.
Who bawl, and swear, and make a fuss,
　And such dull stories tell,
First rate at Poonah—but with us
　They don't go very well.
　　　Sing *Lalleballoo, &c.*

The whole is such a grand mistake.
　Of purse pride and red tape,
That all should do their best, to make
　Its form a wholesome shape.
The Company's done up, and won't
　Say much more now about it,
So long live India—if it don't
　The world can roll without it.
　　　Sing *Lalleballoo, &c.*

CANTON.

Oh! what a place is this capital celestial,
    Never to be equalled in the memory of man;
Different from any in the universe terrestrial,
    Unless you go a little further nor'ard to Japan.
Crowds of people, hustle, bustle, things on bamboo carrying,
Some on coffin-pigeon bound, and others bent on marrying ;
Women toddling on their little ten toes very funnily,
Fortune-tellers telling fools where hidden hoards of money lie.

Oh! what a city, what a charivari wonderful,
    Rushing, crushing—crying, lying—all at once,
With their shortly shaven heads of every blessed blunder full,
    Cupidity, stupidity, half sage, half dunce.
Pastry-cooks, and men with books, and shoemakers all travelling,
Conjurors, and necromancers, future knots unravelling ;
Barber's shops for shaving crops, and strops that need no lathering,
Sing-song fighters, letter writers, altogether gathering.

Oh! what a lot of shops of ivory and lacquer ware,
    Cups and balls, and silks and shawls, and flowers and fans!
Jars of China crackle rare, and fireworks and cracker ware,
    Dragon-boats, and paper-coats, and pots and pans.
Here's a travelling eating-house entirely of bamboo made,
Where the cook half naked plies his pig, and duck, and samshoo trade.
Dogs and frogs, and rats and bats, and fish of figure comical,
Pickled snails, and pussy's tails, all richly gastronomical.

Oh! what antiquity—here's compasses magnetical,
    Used by them before we'd any ships upon the ocean,
Books and prints, sold ages since, by men peripatetical,
    When of Guttenburg and Caxton no one had a notion.
Flower-gardens, where Fankweis like Villikins are vallaking,
Travelling apothecaries to their patients tallaking.
(That's to suit my style of verse, which little more than gab I call,
'Cause the metre ought to end in rhymes all trysyllabical.)

Oh! what a row, what a rumpus and a rioting,
    Cavilling and travelling—unravelling their stores,
Hogs and frogs, and puppy dogs: you never can be quiet in
    Such a city—what a pity they're such noisy bores.
Living all as thickly packed as rabbits in a burrow there,
Streets so narrow, here's a barrow taking up the thoroughfare ;
Next we meet the travelling seat of some quack doctor musical,
Selling potions, pills and lotions, which of no great use I call.

Oh! what a rapid singer, I am not his match at all,
    But to show you Canton, in his style I'll try;
I have done my very best, but if you cannot catch it all,
    Please to recollect 'tis *you* in fault, *not I.*

THE WAR WITH CHINA:
OUR OWN NOTIONS OF IT BEFORE WE WENT THERE.

WE are not about to enter into a political controversy. We leave that exciting task to the wrangling editors of newspapers, the writers of stitched pamphlets without covers, and the race of quarrelsome gentlemen who squabble after dinner during that very bearish time which custom has appropriated to such verbal engagements, when old port, ring chips, Derby and Dizzy, clusters of grapes tied together with sawdusty thread, *Mirabelles de Metz*, sponge-cake, cut-glass and claret, are presumed to be proper and equivalent substitutes for the presence of the fairer portion of the creation. We are not going to bring forward any statistics of tea, silk, and opium; neither can we give the reader any information upon the state of the workhouses, or names of the boards of guardians in various parishes pertaining to the Canton, Macao, or Chusan unions. But we do not see why we should not say *our* few words upon the Chinese Question, which seems so troublesome to answer; the more so as we are an ardent admirer of the refreshing beverage; in addition, adore little feet and ivory carvings; and especially lean to the old blue-pattern plates and dishes.

When we first heard there was a prospect of a war with China, we regarded it as a rumour of extreme eccentricity—a piece of exquisite fun, replete with droll actions and engagements. The impressions of the man are composed of the same elements as the ideas of childhood, although circumstance exerts a slight alteration in their affinity; and we could not entirely divest ourselves of the thoughts we were accustomed to link with "China and the Chinese," when the Arabian Nights' Entertainments—every word of whose gorgeous illusions we received as Gospel—ranked far above the productions of Shakspere, Byron, or Scott, in our immature conception. Nor was the picture we formed of China conjured up by our own minds alone. We had the opportunity of referring to a valuable series of tea-canisters on the shelves of a neighbouring grocer, who opened his shop as the "China Tea Company," hung balloons in his windows, japanned his drawers, sold tea-chests for rabbit-hutches, and had a strange squat figure seated in the centre of the four-shilling Bohea compartment, that wagged its head and tongue all day long at the gazers whom its antics attracted to flatten their noses against his panes of glass. From the aforesaid canisters we were enabled to glean much valuable pictorial information respecting the domestic manners of the Chinese. Probably, we might have studied the subject more deeply, but fate willed otherwise. The concern failed, the shop was closed, and the "Company" ran off in the middle of the night, no one knew whither, and we believe no one cared, except those who had demands upon the establishment. We only wondered what effect the defalcation had upon the funds of the Celestial Empire.

We were a long time bringing ourselves to think that the Chinese were a nation of men and women; in fact, human beings, who thought, moved, and acted in a manner similar to ourselves. We much more readily inclined to the opinion that they were a race of supernatural animated ornaments, who wore inverted basins for head-dresses, and kept odd-shaped dragons and monsters, all claws and crockery, for

their domestic animals. We pictured to ourselves their abodes made
of porcelain, painted all sorts of colours, and thatched with rice-paper.
Their cities we conjured up as lighted by millions of isinglass
lanterns, which kept perpetually turning round. Their vegetation we
confined to curious strange arborescent productions, with large round
vermilion balls for fruit, growing naturally in a state of the highest
varnish; and we could almost see their public roads, buildings, and
fortifications, all constructed of *papier-mâché*, gaily japanned. If war
had been declared at that period, we should not have been much
astonished to have found some morning that all the China ornaments
in England had walked off spontaneously to take up the cause of their
country, and fight in its defence. These ideas continued in full force
with us for some long period, until a series of Eastern spectacles, which
it was our luck to witness at the theatres, turned the current of our
minds into another channel. For the first time we then became aware
that real living beings formed the population of the country belonging
to the sun's intimate connection; but even these differed from other
people. They wore odd six-angled hats, a species of painted convol-
vulus-shaped gossamers, with bells hung round them; they danced
strange figures, with the forefingers of each hand elevated to the level
of their ears; they allowed their mustachios to grow until they trailed
upon the ground; and, in their stage encounters, one English sailor
generally fought twelve at once, all of whom he finally put to flight,
having cut off their pigtails, or whirled them round by these appendages,
like horizontal bandalores, until they were choked. And is it true, we
asked ourselves, that the Government is seriously thinking of going to
war with these grotesque beings? What huge fun we immediately
foresaw in the encounter; what a realization of the scenes in *Aladdin*
and the *Bronze Horse*, to say nothing of *The Illustrious Stranger* and
Zazezizozu, of former times, at Covent Garden, and the more recent
Ba-ta-clan, of the *Bouffes* in Paris! And our great men-of-war and
gun-boats were sailing out, actually and literally sailing out, to engage
with their junks—those odd constructions of thin painted laths, strips
of red cloth, and reed masts with tea-leaf sails, that we could almost
have built from imagination! Why, we should have thought that one
small cannon-ball would have crashed through twenty of them at once,
splintering and smashing them in all directions. It appeared perfectly
cowardly in our nation to think for an instant of attacking in reality
a set of poor scaramouches who resided in inverted tea-cups on a large
scale, lived on paper shavings and fried silkworms, built pagodas like
magnified card houses, and whose most inspiring war-music was com-
prised in a band of copper stew-pans. At length we heard that there
really had been a skirmish, and that one of their great admirals, who
rejoiced in the high-sounding and aristocratic appellation of Wang, had
written a letter, or published a document, or something of the kind.
We should very much like to have seen that document. We will be
bound it was something exquisitely comic, written with various inks,
commencing at the bottom, and filled with characters from the endless
alphabet which adorns the invoices of tea-chests and cakes of Indian
ink. But—ha! ha! ha!—you can scarcely help smiling at the bare
idea, the mere fact of their even daring to expostulate; they, of whom
we should have conceived one halfpenny squib would have put to

flight an army; they, whose cannon we thought must be varnished pasteboard, and whose fortifications carved ivory; they, whose only commerce consisted, independently of their tea, in pearl card-counters and books of gaudy birds and flowers, or ornaments like miniature trunks of trees with distorted spines, carved into human heads at the top; these odd creatures had remonstrated with England. How very ridiculous!

Why it is that the whole empire has not, long before this, been blown entirely to atoms by our guns, we are at a loss to conceive. British humanity must be the only obstacle to such a performance. But, if they are still insolent, we counsel instant and unmitigated annihilation of the whole of them; for what would all our former glories avail us, in the page of history, if we were finally jockeyed by a tribe of nodding mandarins, crockery-baking savages, painters of rice-paper, and manufacturers of chop-sticks and feather fans?

By way of a rider, we subjoin the last expresses from the Celestial Empire, by our own private electro-galvanic communication. As this rapid means of transmission carries despatches so fast that we generally get them before they are written, we are enabled to be considerably in advance of the common daily journals, more especially as we have obtained news up to next Midsummer.

The most important paper which has come to hand is the *Pekin Sunday Times*. It appears that "the fortifications for surrounding the city are progressing rapidly; but that the Government have determined upon building the ramparts of japanned canvass and bamboo rods, instead of pounded rice, which was thought too fragile to resist the attacks of the English barbarians. Some handsome porcelain guns have been placed upon the walls, with a proportionate number of carved ivory balls, elaborately cut one inside the other. These, it is presumed, will split upon firing, and produce incalculable mischief and confusion. Within the gates a frightful magazine of gilt crackers and other fireworks has been erected, which, in the event of the barbarians penetrating the fortifications, will be exploded one after another to terrify them into fits, when they will be easily captured. This precaution has scarcely been thought necessary by some of the mandarins, as their great artist, Ching, has covered the external joss-house with frantic figures, that must strike terror to the souls of all beholders. Gilt paper has also been kept burning upon altars of holy clay at every practicable point of the defences, which it is hardly thought the barbarians will have the hardihood to approach; and the sacred ducks of Fan-qui have been turned loose in the river, to retard the progress of the infidel fleet.

"During the storm of last week the portcullis which had been placed in the northern gate, and was composed of solid rice-paper, with cross-bars of chop-sticks, was much damaged. It is now under repair, and will be coated entirely with tea-chest lead, to render it perfectly impregnable. The whole of the household troops and body-guard of the Emperor have also received new accoutrements of tin-foil and painted isinglass. They have likewise been armed with japanned bladders, containing peas and lychee-stones, which produce a terrific sound upon the least motion.

"An Englishman has been gallantly captured this morning, in a

small boat, by one of our armed junks. He will eat his eyes in the
palace court this afternoon ; and then, being enclosed in soft porcelain,
will be baked to form a statue for the new pagoda at Bo-Lung, the first
stone of which was laid by the late Emperor, to celebrate his victory
over the rude northern islanders."

"Canton.

"The Emperor has issued two following chops to the Hong merchants,
forbidding them to assist or correspond with the barbarians, under
pain of having their finger-nails drawn out, and rings put in their
eyelids. Howqua resists the order ; and it is the intention of Pee-
kwee, should he remain obstinate, to recommend his being pounded up
with broken crockery, and packed in Chinese catty packages, to be
forwarded, as an example, to the Tea-Mandarin Phi-Lips, of the street
of the monarch William, near the Bridge of Lon-Don.

"An English flag, stolen by a deserter from Chusan, will be formally
insulted to-morrow in the market-place by the Emperor and his court.
Derisive grimaces will be made at it by the mandarins of the sixth
class ; and it will subsequently be hoisted, in scorn, to blow at the
mercy of the winds upon the summit of the palace, within sight of the
barbarians.

"An English soldier, despatched by the barbarians on a mission of
peace, was dispatched by our people on his arrival."